"It was fun, Livvy. Ap
yourself down the scr

She felt her eyes fill with t
the same, the freedom from the burden of everyone
watching their words so they didn't reopen the
emotional wounds or poke the sleeping tiger. That was
why hardly anybody at Yoxburgh Park Hospital knew
her medical history, and why she hadn't told Matt.

"You're right, it was fun, but we're back now."

"Yes, we're back. Amber insisted on sleeping with me
last night, and Charlie woke up at four crying because
he'd wet the bed. Definitely back. And it feels *good* to
be back, I really missed them, but I'm very, very glad I
went away, too, and I'm glad you were there with me."

She smiled at him. "I'm glad, too. Still, it's over now."
Odd, how that made her feel sad. It wasn't as if
anything had really happened. Just a couple of kisses,
some shared banter, the odd hug. How could she miss
that so much?

"It doesn't have to be over," he said, after a long pause.

Dear Reader,

Well, I finally got there, and this is my 100th book! And I thought, because I hate a loose end, that it would be lovely to go back twenty-eight years to where it all started and give Livvy, the daughter of Oliver and Bron, my first ever hero and heroine, her own story. Livvy, their love child from a fleeting affair at a conference, was around eighteen months old at the start of *Relative Ethics*, which makes her twenty-nine now and old enough to be a registrar. Great, I thought, I'll give her a happy, lighthearted little story—and then my editor said, "What's her conflict?" and that all got swept under the carpet!

My editor was absolutely right, of course, as usual (!), so here it is, Livvy's not-so-lighthearted but definitely heartfelt love affair with a single father broken by grief but ready to love again. He has so much to offer her, so much tenderness and understanding that he gives her the inner strength to dare to love him, to dream of a future and to overcome her past and move on with him and his beautiful little children as part of their family.

It was such a joy to give them their happy ending, and I don't think I've ever had a couple so in need of happiness and so very worthy of it. I hope you love them both as much as I do.

Here it is, with my love,

Caroline x

A SINGLE DAD
TO HEAL HER HEART

———

CAROLINE ANDERSON

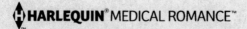
HARLEQUIN® MEDICAL ROMANCE™

Recycling programs
for this product may
not exist in your area.

ISBN-13: 978-1-335-64147-2

A Single Dad to Heal Her Heart

First North American Publication 2019

Copyright © 2019 by Caroline Anderson

This edition published by arrangement with Harlequin Books S.A.

For questions and comments about the quality of this book, please contact us at CustomerService@Harlequin.com.

® and TM are trademarks of Harlequin Enterprises Limited or its corporate affiliates. Trademarks indicated with ® are registered in the United States Patent and Trademark Office, the Canadian Intellectual Property Office and in other countries.

Printed in U.S.A.

We hope you've enjoyed
A Single Dad to Heal Her Heart,
Caroline Anderson's 100th book!

Books by Caroline Anderson

Harlequin Medical Romance

Hope Children's Hospital
One Night, One Unexpected Miracle

Yoxburgh Park Hospital

From Christmas to Eternity
The Secret in His Heart
Risk of a Lifetime
Their Meant-to-Be Baby
The Midwife's Longed-For Baby
Bound by Their Babies
Their Own Little Miracle

Harlequin Romance

The Valtieri Baby
Snowed in with the Billionaire
Best Friend to Wife and Mother?

Visit the Author Profile page
at Harlequin.com for more titles.

For Ali, without whose skill and perseverance with my knotted muscles none of my recent books would have ever been written, and whose extraordinary frankness and generosity in sharing her cancer journey have made it possible for me to write Livvy's story. I can't thank you enough for all you've done for me. I just wish I could give you your happy ending. xxx

CHAPTER ONE

'Wow, LOOK AT that glorious view!'

Stifling her impatience, Livvy glanced back across the scree slope to the valley floor stretched out below them, the late spring grass a splash of vivid green. In the distance Buttermere lay like a gleaming mirror, the bleak slate hills behind it rich purple in the sun.

And between her and the view—admittedly glorious—was Matt, dawdling his way up the winding, rocky path and driving her nuts because it was the last day of their team-building exercise in Cumbria and there was a trophy at stake.

They'd been there since Friday, four teams all in some way connected to the emergency department of Yoxburgh Park Hospital; Sam and Vicky from the ED, Dan and Lucy from Orthopaedics, and Ed and Beth from Paediatrics, which had left her and Matt as the Trauma team.

She'd only started at the hospital a few weeks ago and she'd met him a few times fleetingly when he'd come down to the ED, but ever since they'd arrived at the lodge and sat down together to decide who would be in each team, she and Matt had seemed a natural fit.

'Are you OK with that?' she'd asked at the time, and he'd nodded, his grin a little cheeky.

'Yeah, suits me. You're small enough that I can pick you up if you dawdle.'

'I don't dawdle, and you'd better not!'

'Don't worry, Livvy, I think I can just about keep up with you,' he'd said drily, and he had, seemingly effortlessly. They'd tackled all manner of challenges, and he'd been witty, mischievous, not above cheating and game for anything Sam threw at them.

Until now. Now, with everything to play for, he was stopping to admire the view?

Yes, it was beautiful, and if they had time she'd stop and drink it in, but they didn't because so far the four teams were neck and neck, so the first to the summit of Haystacks would take the crown. And Matt was trailing.

Deliberately?

'Are you dawdling on purpose or just studying my backside?' she asked, hands on hips and her head cocked to one side, and he stopped just below her, a smile playing around that really rather gorgeous mouth that she was itching to kiss.

He took a step closer, curling his hands around her hips and sending shivers of something interesting through her. They were standing eye to eye, and his mouth was so close now...

His smile widened, crows' feet bracketing those laughing eyes the colour of the slate that surrounded them, and he shook his head slowly from side to side.

'Cute though it is, and it has been worth watching, I'll admit, I was actually studying the scenery then.' The smile faded, replaced by awe. 'Stop and look around you, Livvy, just for a moment. It's so beautiful and you're missing it—and anyway, it's only supposed to be fun!'

She sighed, knowing he was right, but still impatient. 'I know, but we can't let Sam catch us now, we'll never hear the end of it. We can look on the way back when we've won.'

He shook his head again and laughed. 'You're so competitive. Just be careful, that edge is unstable. Why don't you let me go first?'

She laughed at him and took a step backwards out of reach. 'What, to slow me down?

No way. And besides, I'm always careful,' she threw over her shoulder as she turned, and then she took another step and the ground vanished beneath her feet...

'Livvy—!'

He lunged for her, his fingers brushing her flailing arm, but she was gone before he could grab her, her scream slicing the air as she fell. And then the scream stopped abruptly, leaving just a fading echo, and his blood ran cold.

She was below him, lying like a rag doll against a rock, crumpled and motionless, and for a moment he was frozen.

No. Please, God, no...

'Livvy, I'm coming. Hang on,' he yelled, and scanned the slope, found a safe route that wouldn't send more rocks showering down on her and scrambled down, half running, half sliding across the shale. Fast, but not too fast. Not so fast that he'd put himself in danger, too, because that wouldn't help either of them.

As he got closer he could see her shoulders heaving, as if she was fighting for breath, and then as he got to her side she sucked in a small breath, rolled onto her back and started to pant jerkily, and his legs turned to jelly.

She was breathing. Not well, but she wasn't dead...

He took her hand and gripped it gently. 'It's OK, Livvy, I'm here, I've got you. You're OK now. Just keep breathing, nice and slow. That's it. Well done.'

Her eyes locked on his, and after a moment her breathing steadied, and he felt his shoulders drop with relief.

'What—happened? Can't—breathe...'

'Just take it steady, you'll recover soon,' he said, his voice calm, his heart still pounding and his mind running through all the things that might be damaged. Starting with her head... 'I think you've been winded. Stay there a minute—'

'Can't. I need to sit up.'

He gritted his teeth. 'OK, but don't do it if you think you've got any other injuries.'

'No. Haven't,' she said, and she struggled up into a sitting position and propped herself against the rock that had stopped her fall.

'Ah—!'

'OK?'

She nodded, shifting slightly, her breathing slowing, and she closed her eyes briefly.

'Yeah. That's better. The path just—went.'

So she remembered that, at least. '"I'm always careful",' he quoted drily, and she laughed weakly as relief kicked in.

'Well, nobody's—perfect,' she said after

a moment, and then her eyes welled and he reached out a hand and brushed the soft blond hair back from her face with fingers that weren't quite steady, scanning her face for bruises.

'Are you OK now? You scared me half to death.'

She met his eyes with a wry smile, and for once the sparkle in her eyes wasn't mischief. 'That depends on your—definition of OK. I'm alive, I can breathe—just, I can feel everything, I can move, so yeah—I guess I'm OK. Do I hurt? Oh, yeah. These rocks are hard.'

'I'm sure. Don't move. Let me check you over.'

'You just want to get your hands on me,' she quipped, her breath still catching.

'Yeah, right,' he said lightly, trying not to think about that right now because however true it might be, he could see she was in pain. He simply wanted to be sure she didn't have any life-threatening injuries and then maybe his heart could slow down a bit. 'Why don't you let me do my job?' he added gently, trying to stick to business.

'Yes, Doctor.'

'Well, at least you can remember that. How many fingers am I holding up?'

'Twelve.'

He tried to glare at her but it was too hard so he just laughed, told her to co-operate and carried on, checking her pupils, making her follow his finger, feeling her scalp for any sign of a head injury.

Please don't have a head injury...

'My head's fine. It's my ribs that hurt.'

So he turned his attention to her body, checking for anything that could be a worry because she'd hit that rock hard and a punctured lung could kill her. He squeezed her rib-cage gently.

'Does that feel OK?'

'Sort of. It's tender, but it's not catching any more when I breathe and I can't feel any grating when you spring them, so I don't think I broke any ribs,' she said, taking it seriously at last. 'I thought I had an elephant on my chest. I had no idea being winded was so damn scary.'

'Oh, yeah. I've only ever been winded once, when I fell out of a tree. I must have been six or seven, but I remember it very clearly. I thought I was dying.'

She nodded, then looked away again, just as they heard a slither of shale and Sam appeared at their sides.

'How is she?' he asked tightly.

'Lippy and opinionated but apparently OK,

as far as I've checked. She was winded. At least it shut her up for a moment.'

Sam chuckled, but Matt could see the relief in his eyes. 'Now there's a miracle.'

'Excuse me, I am here, you know,' she said, shifting into a better position, and Sam looked down at her and grinned.

'So you are. Good job, too, we don't need to lose a promising young registrar, we're pushed enough,' he said drily, and sat down. 'Why don't you shut up and let him finish so we can get on?' he added, and Matt laughed. As if…

'Any back pain?' he asked, but she just gave him a wry look.

'No more than you'd expect after rolling down a scree slope and slamming into a rock, but at least it stopped me rolling all the way down,' she said, trying to get to her feet, but he put a hand on her shoulder and held her down.

'I'm not done—'

She tipped her head back and fixed him with a determined look. 'Yeah, you are. I'm fine, Matt. I just need to get up because there are rocks sticking into me all over the place and I could do without that. You might need to give me a hand up.'

He held his hand out but let her do the work. She'd stop instinctively as soon as anything felt wrong, but he was horribly conscious that he hadn't ruled out all manner of injuries that might be lurking silently, but that was fine, he had no intention of taking his eyes off her for the rest of the day.

She winced slightly, but she was on her feet.

'How's that feel?'

'Better now I'm off the rocks. Did you see what happened? Did I step off the edge, or did it crumble?'

He snorted. 'No, it crumbled. I told you the edge was unstable, but did you listen? Of course not. You were in too much of a hurry. When you weren't walking backwards, that is.'

'Only one step—'

'I'll give you one step,' he growled. 'So, are you OK to go on?'

'Of course I am. You seriously think I'm going to give up now just because of this?'

'You might as well. I don't get beaten,' Sam said, getting to his feet, and she laughed in his face.

'We'll see about that,' she retorted, stabbing him in the chest with her finger, then she took a step and yelped.

Matt frowned. 'What?'

'My ankle.' She tried again, and winced. 'Rats. I can't weight-bear on it. I must have turned it when the path gave way.'

'Well, that's just upped my chances,' Sam said with a grin, and Matt rolled his eyes.

'You two are a nightmare. Right, let's get you off here and have a better look at that.'

Livvy flexed her ankle again and regretted it. She was so mad with herself, and she was hideously aware that it could have been much, much worse. If it had been her head against that rock instead of her chest…

After all she'd been through, that she could have died from a moment's lack of concentration was ridiculous. She'd meant what she'd said about being careful. She was always careful, meticulous with her lifestyle, fastidious about what she ate, how much she exercised— she woke every morning ready to tackle whatever the day brought, because *whatever* it brought she had at least been granted the chance to deal with it, and she never stopped being aware of that glorious gift.

And now, after the physical and emotional roller coaster of the last five years, she'd nearly thrown it all away.

Stupid. Stupid, stupid, stupid.

'OK?'

She nodded, her teeth gritted, because her ankle was definitely not OK and the rest of her body wasn't far behind. She was going to have some stunning bruises to show for this. What an idiot.

They carried her carefully across the loose rock slope to where the others were waiting, clustering round her and looking concerned as they set her on her feet, and she felt silly and horribly embarrassed.

And annoyed, because she'd been really looking forward to climbing up Haystacks and there was no way she was going up it now, and she couldn't see how she could get down, either, so one way or another she was going to miss out on the climb and coincidentally cause the others a whole world of aggravation.

Either that or just sit there and let them pick her up on the way back.

Whatever, they'd be worried about her, Matt especially since he'd seen her fall, and she felt awful now for scaring him. Scaring all of them, and putting a dampener on the whole trip.

'Sorry, guys,' she said humbly. 'That was really stupid.'

'It was an accident. They happen,' Dan said calmly, but Matt just snorted and turned away. Because he was angry with her? Maybe, and she felt like the sun had gone in.

'Want me to look at it?'

'It's fine, Dan. It's only a sprain and anyway I'm not taking my boot off.'

'OK. Just keep your weight off it.'

'I can't do anything else,' she said in disgust, and lowered herself gingerly onto a handy rock.

'So what now?' Matt asked, still not looking at her.

She followed the direction of his gaze and traced the rough path that seemed to wind endlessly down until it met the track that led to the car park. Funny, it didn't look so beautiful now. It just looked a long, long way away.

'We'll carry her down,' Sam said.

'No, you won't. You've got to finish the challenge!' she protested, but Sam shrugged.

'Well, we can't leave you here, Livvy.'

'Yes, you can. I'll be fine. I'm not ruining anyone's day just because I was an idiot. Please, all of you, go on up and I'll wait here. I might even work my way down. If I take my time I'll be fine. I can go down on my bottom.'

'No,' Matt chipped in, turning round at last, his expression implacable. 'I'll take you back. Our team's out, anyway.'

'Are you sure?' Sam asked him, but she shook her head, really unhappy now.

'Matt, I can't let you do that. You were looking forward to it!'

He just smiled, his eyes softening at last. 'It'll keep. It's millions of years old, Livvy. It's not like it's going anywhere. I can climb it another time.'

'But—'

His tone firmed. 'But nothing. We're team-mates, and we stick together, and it's what we're doing. End of.'

She rolled her eyes. 'Are you always this bossy?'

'Absolutely. Ed, can I borrow the car?'

Ed nodded and delved in his pocket and tossed him the keys. 'Mind you don't crash it. Annie'll kill us both.'

'I'll do my best,' he said mildly. 'Go on, you guys, go and have your climb and I'll take Livvy back and come and get you when you're done. Call me when you hit the track.'

'Will do—and no more stunts, Henderson, we need you in one piece!' Sam said as they headed off, leaving her alone with Matt.

He laughed and shook his head in disbelief.

'I can't believe I'm so stupid.'

She looked up at him, her face puzzled. '*You* are?'

'Yes, me. I've spent the last three days trying to work out who you remind me of, and it's just clicked. You're Oliver Henderson's daughter, aren't you? It's so blindingly obvious I can't believe I didn't see it. You're the spitting image of him.'

'Do you know him?'

He perched on a rock in front of her so she didn't have to tilt her head. 'Yes, I was his registrar, years ago. He's a great guy. I'm very fond of him, and your mother. How are they both?'

'Fine. Doing really well. He's about to turn sixty, but he doesn't look it and he's got no plans to retire and nor has Mum.'

'I'm not surprised. They're very dedicated.'

'They are. Dad just loves surgery, and Mum would be bored to bits without the cut and thrust of ED, so I can't see them retiring until they're forced, frankly! So, when were you at the Audley Memorial? I must have been at uni or I'd remember you, unless you're much older than you look.'

He chuckled. 'I'm thirty-six now and I was twenty-seven, so that's—wow, nine years ago.'

'So I must have been twenty then, which explains it, because I didn't come home a lot in those days. I had a busy social life at uni, and it was a long way from Bristol to Suffolk.'

'Yes, it is. Give them my love when you speak to them.'

'I will. I'll call them later today.'

'So, how are we going to do this?' he asked quietly, getting back to the core business, and she shrugged.

'I have no idea. I can't hop all the way down, but I can't walk on it either, so it looks like the bottom shuffle thing.'

'Or I can carry you,' he suggested, knowing she'd argue.

'How? Don't be ridiculous, it's not necessary. And anyway, I weigh too much.'

He laughed at that, because she hardly came up to his chin and, sure, she was strong, but she definitely wasn't heavy, he knew that because he and Sam had already carried her to the path. He got to his feet.

'Come on, then, sling your arm round my neck and let's see how we get on with assisted hopping.'

Slowly, was the answer. He had to stoop, of course, because she was too short to reach his shoulder otherwise, and after a while they had to change sides, but she said it hurt her ribs, which left only one option.

He stopped and went down on one knee.

'Are you proposing to me?' she joked, and it was so unexpected he laughed. Ish.

'Very funny. Get on my back.'

'I can't!'

'Why?'

'Because I'm not five and I'll feel like an idiot!'

He straightened up, unable to stifle the laugh. 'You just fell off the path!' he said, and she swatted him, half cross, half laughing, and he couldn't help himself. He gathered her into his arms, hugged her very gently and brushed the hair away from her eyes as he smiled ruefully down at her.

'I'm sorry. That was mean.'

'Yes, it was. I feel silly enough without you laughing at me.'

'Yeah, I know. I'm sorry,' he said again, and then because he'd been aching to do it for days and because she was just there, her face tipped up to his, her clear blue eyes rueful and apologetic and frustrated, he bent his head and touched his lips to hers.

It was only meant to be fleeting, just a brush of his mouth against hers, but the tension that had been sizzling between them since they'd arrived on Friday morning suddenly escalated, and when her mouth softened under his he felt a surge of something he hadn't felt for two years, something he'd thought he'd never feel again.

Not lust. It wasn't lust. That he would have understood. Expected, even, after so long. But this was tenderness, yearning, a deep ache for something more, something meaningful and fulfilling, something he'd lost, and it stopped him in his tracks.

What was he doing?

He pulled away and cleared his throat.

'Come on, let's get you down to the bottom and I'll go and get the car and come back for you. And I *will* carry you, because frankly it'll be easier for both of us and if I don't get you off this mountain safely your father'll kill me.'

He turned his back on her, knelt down again and told her to get on, and after a moment's hesitation, when he could almost hear her fighting her instincts, she leant into him, wrapped her arms round his neck and let him hoist her up onto his back.

He wrapped her legs round his waist and straightened up with a little lurch, and she gave a tiny shriek that morphed into a giggle.

'This is ridiculous,' she said, and he started to laugh.

Her arms tightened round his throat. 'Don't mock me.'

'I'm not mocking you, I promise,' he said, stifling the laugh, and she loosened her arms around his neck and rested her head against his with a sigh.

'I'm so sorry I messed up your day,' she murmured in his ear, and the drift of her warm breath teased his skin and the feelings he'd thought he'd suppressed roared into life again.

'Don't be,' he said gruffly, trying not to think about his hands locked together under her bottom. Her undoubtedly very, very cute bottom. 'It was just an accident. So, tell me, why trauma?' he asked to distract himself. 'Why not general surgery, like your father?'

'That's probably Mum's influence, and surgery's still an option, but I'm undecided about it, and trauma's a nice high-octane job.'

He chuckled. 'High-octane, sure, but I'm not sure I'd call it nice, especially the surgery. It can get pretty gory.'

'So why did *you* choose it?'

'I don't know. Probably your father's influence. I always wanted to be a surgeon, and when I was his registrar we had some interesting trauma cases and it just reeled me in. Yes, it's gory, but it's very gratifying when you can offer someone who's been badly injured a better outcome.'

'I would have thought you'd have been in London, then. That's where a lot of the trauma cases are. More scope?'

He felt his heart hitch. 'Yeah, well, I've done London, and frankly in the year and a half I've been in Yoxburgh there's been plenty to keep me busy.'

More than enough, and nothing to do with his job. Not that he was going into details. He didn't want to let reality intrude on a weekend that had been like a breath of fresh air after the roller coaster of the last two years, but that was all it was, a breath of fresh air, and it was going nowhere, he knew that, because there simply wasn't room in his life for a relationship, however appealing. And anyway, there was an embargo on personal stuff this weekend, so he changed the subject.

'Are you OK there? I'm not hurting you?'

'No. It's a bit sore, but it's better than walking. How about you?'

'I'm fine. We're nearly there, anyway. Not long now.'

Frankly, it couldn't be soon enough because, apart from being racked with guilt, she was swamped with feelings that were so unexpected she didn't know how to deal with them.

It shouldn't have surprised her that he'd given up his chance of a climb to get her safely back down, because over the last three days he'd proved himself to be tough and determined and a brilliant team player.

Not that he didn't know how to have fun. They'd had plenty of that, and she hadn't laughed so much in ages.

They'd been teasing and flirting for most of the time, too, but she hadn't expected him to act on it and his gentle kiss just now had brought all sorts of unexpected feelings rushing to the surface. Not to mention his hands locked together under her bottom, propping her up. They must be numb by now, and she had another pang of guilt.

'Are you sure you're OK, Matt?'

'I'm fine,' he said, and then they hit the track and he unlocked his hands and braced her as she slid down and put her feet on the ground.

He flexed his hands and shoulders and she watched the muscles roll under his damp T-shirt as he turned to her. 'I won't be long. Will you be all right?'

She lowered herself to a rock and dragged her eyes off his shoulders. 'I'll be fine. There's no rush. I'll just sit here and look at the view,' she told him with a wry smile.

Mostly of him, as he turned away and headed down the track towards the farm at the end where the car was parked.

She studied him, his strong, firm stride, the straight back, his arms hanging loose and relaxed from those broad shoulders. Broad, solid, dependable. And sexy.

Very, very sexy.

Would they see each other again once they

were back? She didn't think so, despite this sizzle between them all weekend, because there was something about him, some reserve in his eyes, and when he'd kissed her he'd pulled away.

Would he have done that if he intended to follow through? Probably not, and she still didn't feel ready for a relationship anyway after all she'd been through, but if nothing else they were good friends now and she'd known from that first day that she could rely on him.

He had a rock-solid dependability, carefully hidden under a lot of jokes and laughter, and if she had to be in this fix, she couldn't have asked for a better person to help her out of it.

She just wished she hadn't made it necessary.

'We need to get this boot off.'

He'd propped her up on a sun lounger on the deck outside the lodge, and he was perched on the end by her feet, wondering how to remove it without hurting her.

'They're pretty old,' she offered. 'I don't mind if you need to cut it off.'

He shook his head. 'I don't think I will. I'll take the lace out and see how we get on.'

He unthreaded it, peeled back the tongue as

far as it would go and slid his fingers carefully inside. 'How's that feel?'

'Not too bad. A bit easier now you've undone the lace.'

'Let's just see what happens if I try and ease your foot out. Yell if I hurt you.'

She gave a stifled snort. 'Don't worry, I will,' she said drily, and he looked up and met those gorgeous clear blue eyes and saw trust in them. He hoped it wasn't unfounded.

'Right, here goes,' he said, and gently cupping his hand under her ankle to support it, he eased the boot away.

She made a tiny whimper at one point, but nothing more, and then it was off and he lowered her foot carefully onto a pillow. 'How's that feel?'

Her breath sighed out. 'Better. Thank you.'

'Don't thank me, I haven't prodded it yet,' he said drily, and began to feel his way carefully around the joint, testing the integrity of the ligaments.

'Ow.'

'Sorry.' He prodded a little more, feeling carefully for any displacement, but if there was it was slight. 'I don't think it's fractured, and it doesn't feel displaced, so I think it's probably only a slight ligament tear. You need an X-ray, though.'

'It can wait till we get back, can't it?'

He nodded. 'I think so. There's not much else going on with it, I don't think, but we'll get Dan to look at it when he comes back just to be on the safe side. In the meantime I'll get you some ice and I can strap it, if you like. That should help.'

'Please. And I could kill a cup of green tea—oh, and a banana, if there's one left,' she said, throwing a grin over her shoulder as he headed for the kitchen, and he gave a grunt of laughter.

'I get the distinct impression you're milking this,' he said drily as he walked away, and he put the kettle on, discovered there were no ice cubes, wetted a couple of tea towels and put them in the freezer, and raided the first-aid kit for some physio tape.

'Better?'

She nodded. 'Much.'

It was, hugely better, which wasn't difficult. Her boot had been pressing on the outside of her ankle, and removing it had made a lot of difference. So had the cold pack and the strapping that, considering he was a trauma surgeon and not a physio or an orthopaedic surgeon, was looking very professional. It still shouldn't have happened, though, and she sighed.

'What?'

She shrugged. 'Just—I'm cross with myself. And sorry, because I really thought we had a good chance of winning until I took my eye off the ball, and now I've blown it and ruined your last day.'

He frowned, his eyes serious. 'It's hardly ruined. You're alive, Livvy, and you might not have been. If your head had hit that rock instead of your ribs, it could have been a very different story. I'd take that as a win any day. And it doesn't matter about my climb, or the challenge.'

'Yes, it does, and I still feel guilty. If you'd teamed up with someone else you might have won, but now I've let you down.'

'No, you haven't.'

'Yes, I have! I'm the weak link in the chain, Matt.'

He rolled his eyes. 'You're not weak! There's nothing weak about you.'

'I didn't look where I was going on a narrow rocky path with a crumbling edge. That's pretty weak from where I'm standing.'

'You're sitting. Well, lying, really, technically speaking.'

She was, still propped up on the sun lounger with her ankle wrapped in the thawing tea towel in a plastic bag, a cup of green tea in her hand and a packet of crunchy oat cookies on the table between them because apparently the bananas were finished. Ah, well. She took another cookie and bit into it.

'You're a pedant, did you know that?' she said mildly around the crumbs, and he chuckled, his frown fading.

'It might have been mentioned. How's your ankle now?'

'Cold.'

'Good. How about your ribs?'

'Sore. I might move the ice pack.'

'Here, let me.'

He picked up the makeshift ice pack, turned it over and gestured to her to pull up her T-shirt. She eased it out of the way and he winced.

'Ow. That's a good bruise. Let me feel that.'

'Why, because poking it is going to make it feel so much better?' she said drily, but he just gave her a look that was getting all too familiar and tugged up her T-shirt a little further. And then he frowned and ran his finger across the top of her abdomen from side to side along her scar. Well, one of them.

'What happened? Another accident?'

'Yes, but not my fault, before you say it. I was in a car crash when I was nineteen months old. I had a ruptured spleen and a perforated bowel.'

'Ouch.' He turned his attention back to her ribs and prodded them gently and rather too thoroughly. 'Well, there's nothing displaced,' he said, and she rolled her eyes.

'I could have told you that. I don't have a fracture, Matt.'

'How do you know? It's not possible to be sure.'

She sighed. 'Because I'm inside my body and you're not?'

One eyebrow shot up, his eyes locked briefly with hers and then he let his breath out on what could have been a laugh and tugged her T-shirt back down, and she realised what she'd said.

Colour flooded her face and she groaned. 'Sorry—I didn't mean that quite the way it came out.'

'No, I don't suppose you did.' He got to his feet and picked up his mug, hefting the ice pack in his hand and avoiding her eyes. 'This thing's thawed. I'll get you another one, then I'll make some more coffee and sort my stuff out. Do you want another drink?'

She shook her head, half mortally embarrassed at her off-the-cuff remark, and half tantalised by the idea of Matt's really rather gorgeous body so intimately locked with hers.

'No, I'm fine.'

She heard the door close behind her and

stifled a groan, then dropped her head back against the sun lounger and closed her eyes.

Why had she said that? She'd never be able to look him in the eye again. Idiot. Idiot, idiot, idiot!

But her body was still caught up in the thought, and she didn't know whether to laugh or cry…

CHAPTER TWO

She didn't mean it like that.

Obviously she didn't mean it like that, but the idea was in his head now, the thought of his body buried deep inside hers flooding his senses and driving him crazy.

He closed the kitchen door, put the tea towel back into the freezer, switched the kettle on again and then dropped his head against the cupboard above and growled with frustration.

What was *wrong* with him today? First the kiss, now this?

For the first time since Juliet, he wanted a woman. Not just any woman, but Livvy, apparently, and the thought wouldn't leave him alone.

All he could think about was peeling away her clothes and kissing every inch of her, touching her, stroking her skin, feeling the warmth of her body against his, the hitch in her breath as he touched her more intimately, the heat as he buried himself inside her—and he didn't know how to deal with it.

Should he be feeling like this? It had been two years—two years and a week, to be exact—but was that long enough? He didn't think so, but his body didn't seem to agree with him.

What do I do, Jules? Where do I go from here? I'm not ready for this...

He heard a sound in the living room and opened the door. Livvy was limping across the room, hopping from one piece of furniture to the next and then leaning heavily on it as she hobbled.

'Where are you going?'

'I thought I'd go and lie down for a bit, then maybe pack?'

'Let me give you a hand.'

'I can manage.'

Stubborn woman.

'Of course you can, but only until you run out of furniture.'

He reached her side, took her arm and slung it round his neck and wrapped his other arm round her waist, being careful of her ribs.

'OK?'

She nodded, and as she took a step forward there was a sharp crack and she gasped.

'Was that your ankle?'

'Mmm. Ouch.'

They looked down and she flexed it gingerly. 'Oh. It feels better—like something was hung up.'

'Try putting some weight on it, but carefully.'

She did, and nodded. 'Better. It's still very sore, but that definitely feels better.'

'OK, well, don't push your luck and don't try and weight-bear on it unnecessarily until you've had it X-rayed. Let's get you to your room.'

When they reached the side of the bed he let go carefully and she eased away from him, taking all that wonderful warmth and softness with her. Just as well. Except that instead of sitting down, as he'd expected, she looked up at him, slid her arms round him and hugged him, bringing all that warmth and softness back into intimate contact with his starving, grateful, desperate body.

'Thank you,' she murmured.

His arms closed around her without his permission. 'What for?' he asked, his voice a little strangled.

'Just being you. You've been great the last few days. It's been so much fun—well, till I wrecked it.'

'You didn't wreck it.'

She tipped her head back and their eyes met. 'Yes, I did. Stop being nice, Matt. I know I was an idiot.'

He laughed softly and kissed her without thinking.

Just a brief kiss, nothing passionate or romantic, but still the sort of kiss you'd give a lover, a partner. Someone you were intimate with. And he wasn't intimate with Livvy, and wasn't going to be. He wasn't ready yet, and he had other commitments that had to take priority. Would always have to take priority.

So he straightened up, trying to distance himself when all he wanted was to topple her backwards onto the bed and make love to her, but her eyes had widened, and after an endless moment she reached up, pulled his head gently back down to hers and kissed him.

Properly, this time, her lips parting, her tongue tangling with his, reeling him in, sending his senses into freefall.

He wanted her.

Every cell in his body was screaming for it, for her, for the heat, the passion, the closeness. He could feel her body pressed against his, feel his roaring to life, the ache, the longing in both of them as he kissed her back with all the pent-up need of two years of loneliness and putting himself last.

And then abruptly she let him go and sat down on the bed out of reach.

'Is that your phone?'

Phone?

The ringtone was almost drowned out by his pounding heart, but it dragged him savagely back to reality.

'Um—yeah. Yeah, it is.'

He pulled it out of his pocket, slightly dazed, took a step back and turned away, clearing his throat and groping for a normal voice.

'Hi, Sam. Are you done?'

'Yes—we've just reached the track. How's Livvy?'

Kissing me...

'She's fine. I don't think it's broken. I'll come and get you.' He put the phone back in his pocket and turned back to her without meeting her eyes. 'That was Sam,' he said unnecessarily. 'I'm going to get them. Will you be OK?'

'Of course I will. You go. I'll see you later.'

He nodded, his heart pounding, his body screaming for more, his head all over the place.

What was going on with him? How could he want her so badly?

He had no idea, but he didn't have time to deal with it now, and maybe never. Stifling regret, he picked the keys up and walked out.

* * *

They loaded the car after lunch, did a final sweep of the lodge for missed possessions and set off on the six-hour drive back to Suffolk. She was in the front beside Ed to give her room to stretch her foot out, and Matt was behind her with Sam and Beth, with Lucy, Dan and Vicky in the rear.

She sighed quietly, and Ed shot her a searching look.

'Are you OK?'

She nodded. 'Yes, I'm fine. Well, apart from feeling guilty for getting the best seat and ruining everyone's day.'

'You do a lot of that. Feeling guilty. You don't need to, at least not around me. It took you and Matt out and distracted Sam enough that Beth and I won, so I've got no beef with you,' he told her with a grin, then his smile gentled. 'Livvy, why don't you just close your eyes and rest? You've had a tough day.'

She nodded, wishing again that she hadn't fallen, that she hadn't kissed Matt again in the bedroom and made things awkward, that she was sitting beside him and taking advantage of the last few hours they had together, instead of being in the front with a damaged ankle and a feeling that she'd overstepped the mark with that kiss.

Would he want to see her again? Maybe, maybe not. If his phone hadn't rung, what would have happened? Would they have made love? Maybe, and that surprised her because she didn't do that sort of thing. It hadn't even been on her radar for the last five years, but she'd never fallen into bed with someone she knew so little and certainly not after only three days of casual flirting, but maybe he didn't do that sort of thing either, because when Sam had called him, he couldn't get out fast enough. Had she read him wrong all weekend?

Highly likely, judging from his reaction, although he'd been with her all the way when they'd been kissing—or she thought he had. His body certainly had been, but maybe not his head.

Well, it didn't matter, the moment was gone, the bullet dodged, and it was just as well because there were things he didn't know yet—things she'd have to tell him before this went any further. If it was even going to, and she wasn't sure she was ready for that.

Probably just as well his phone had rung, then.

What was wrong with him? Why was he reacting like this?

She was right in front of him, so close that

the scent of her shampoo, so familiar now, was drifting over him and taunting him just like it had all weekend.

How could he want her like this? He didn't even know her—and three days under Sam's embargo of any personal information or discussion of life back home or in the hospital hadn't helped with that at all. She was still an unknown quantity. And if he knew nothing about her apart from that she was Oliver's daughter, she also knew nothing about him, about his life, his family, his motivations, his commitments.

He could have told her, could have broken the embargo and spilled his guts, but he hadn't wanted to. If he was honest, he'd enjoyed the freedom of simply being himself, without all the baggage that went with it, but there was no way he could take it any further than a mild flirtation without her knowing a whole lot more about him. It wouldn't be fair, it wouldn't be honest, and there was a world of difference between being frugal with the truth and denying the most important things in his life.

And anyway, he had nothing to offer her, nothing that wouldn't be an insult.

He rested his head back and closed his eyes, but she moved her head and the scent drifted towards him again and there was no escape.

* * *

Halfway back they stopped for a drink and a leg stretch. Ed and Sam swapped places, and yet again she wasn't next to Matt, who was now right in the back, as far away from her as he could get. Why hadn't he offered to drive? Was he avoiding her? Maybe, after that excruciatingly embarrassing remark she'd made, not to mention the way she'd kissed him afterwards. She still couldn't believe she'd done it, it was so unlike her to take the initiative, and she'd probably embarrassed the life out of him. Oh, well, they'd be back soon and she'd see then if she was right or not.

Finally Sam pulled up in front of her house and Matt climbed out, retrieved her rucksack and helped her into her house, then paused on the doorstep looking troubled.

'Will you be OK on your own?'

So he *was* avoiding her, or he'd offer to stay with her. Sucking up her disappointment, she straightened her shoulders and plastered a bright smile on her face. 'Yes, I'm fine. I've got friends round the corner if I get stuck.'

'You're sure? No headache, no abdominal pain, no spinal issues? Numbness, tingling anywhere?'

She sighed. 'Matt, I'm *fine*,' she said patiently, and he gave a brief nod.

'OK. Get checked over tomorrow, won't you—or sooner if…?'

He hesitated a moment, his eyes locked with hers, and for a fraction of a second she thought he was going to kiss her, but then he smiled wistfully and reached out and touched her cheek, brushing it lightly with his knuckles. 'It's been a lot of fun. Thank you, Livvy. Take care.'

And with that he turned and walked down the path and got back into the car, and Sam pulled away, leaving her staring after them as they turned the corner and disappeared.

She closed the door with a sigh, hopped into her sitting room, lowered herself carefully onto the sofa and put her foot up.

So that was the end of that, then. So much for hoping something more might come of it. He could have stayed, or offered to come back after Ed had dropped him off, but he hadn't, and all she could do was accept it. Not that she was looking for a relationship, in any way, but it would have been nice to be asked. Nice to be more than just *fun*.

Unless he was…?

Oh, idiot. He was married. Hence the guilt in his eyes, the reluctance, the harmless dalliance that didn't break any vows but just made it a bit more *fun*.

That word again.

She rested her head back, closed her eyes and swallowed her disappointment. She was tired. Tired, confused and sore. That was all. And it wasn't as if anything had really happened...

Her phone rang, and she answered it.

'Hi, Dad. How's things?'

'Fine. How are you? How was the weekend?'

Confusing...

'Great. I'm just back, actually. It was fabulous. Well, until this morning on the way up to Haystacks when I fell off the edge of a path and twisted my ankle.'

'Ouch! Are you all right? How did you get down?'

Fast, but that wasn't what he meant and she wasn't telling them she could have tumbled all the way down to the bottom of the scree slope if it hadn't been for the rock. 'Carefully,' she said with a wry laugh. 'Two of the guys helped me back to the path, and then Matt carried me down. You know him, he's one of your old registrars. Matt Hunter? He's a consultant trauma surgeon at Yoxburgh, and he was my teammate.'

'Matt? Wow,' he said softly, something slightly odd in his voice that puzzled her. 'How is he?'

Even more puzzling. 'He's fine. Why?'

'I just wondered. I haven't seen him since his wife died.'

She felt a slither of cold run down her spine. 'His wife *died*?' she said, her voice hollow, because she'd just worked out he was married, but he wasn't, or at least not any more…

'Yeah. Juliet, and they had two tiny children. She had a brain haemorrhage while we were at a conference, and she didn't make it. I'm sure I told you about it. It must have been two years ago.'

That was Matt? She felt sick. 'You did, I remember. Oh, that's awful. I didn't know it was him. So he's got two little children?'

'Yes, a boy and a girl. They were just babies, really. I suppose Charlie must be nearly three now, and I should think Amber's about to start school, but it was desperately sad. He's a really nice guy—friendly, funny, easygoing, but rock solid and utterly reliable. I'm sure he's a brilliant father.'

Her heart ached for him. 'I'm sure he is.' And it explained the thing she hadn't been able to identify that lurked in the back of his eyes, and the fact that, embargo or not, every night he'd disappeared for a few minutes.

To check the children were OK, and talk to them?

And it also explained why he'd left her this evening rather than come in, and why he'd looked torn about it. Not because he was married, but because he had two little people who would have been missing him.

'So he seemed OK to you?' her father was asking.

Had he?

'Yes, absolutely fine—or I thought so. He didn't say anything about it, but Sam had banned us from talking about home or work. It was all about having a clean slate and not making pre-judgements about each other, but I would never have guessed all that in a million years.'

'No, I don't suppose he'd show it, anyway. He probably wanted to leave it at home. I hear he's an excellent surgeon. He showed huge promise nine years ago, so I'm not surprised he's a consultant now. I think he was only about thirty-four or so when Juliet died, but he'd done a spell with the Helicopter Emergency Medical Service, and by the time she died he was a specialist registrar in a major London trauma unit, poised and ready for a serious consultancy. It's a massive career change for him to move to sleepy Suffolk, but it's obvious why he's done it. I know his family are in the area. Give him our best wishes when you see him again, and tell him we often think about him.'

'I will. So—talking of fathers,' she said, changing the subject because frankly she needed time to let all that lot settle, 'how are the plans for your sixtieth coming on?'

He laughed ruefully. 'I have no idea. Your mother's sorting that out, but I believe we're having a marquee at home and a catered buffet and dancing. Jamie's doing the playlist so goodness knows what the music'll be like, and Abbie and your mother have chosen the menu but I have no idea what's on it. To be honest I'm trying not to think about it because I don't feel that old, so I'm in denial.'

She chuckled softly. 'Well, if it's any consolation, Dad, you don't look it, either, so I'd enjoy your party and go with the flow. So what have you guys been up to over the weekend?'

He let himself in quietly, and found his mother dozing in the family room. He closed the door softly, and she stirred.

'Hi, Mum. I'm home.'

Her eyes blinked open and she smiled. 'Oh, hello, darling. I must have dozed off. Did you have a lovely time?'

He stooped and kissed her cheek and dropped

onto the sofa beside her. 'Great, thanks to you. How've they been?'

'Fine, if a little wearing. Have you been worrying?'

He laughed softly. 'Not really—not about them, more about being so far away. All the what-ifs. You know...'

'Yes, of course I know. I knew you would be, but we've all been fine. They've been as good as gold all weekend. I've only just put them to bed but I'm sure they won't mind if you wake them. I would have kept them up for you but they were shattered. They've been really busy. Amber's drawn you hundreds of pictures, and Charlie's helped me in the garden, and we've been to the beach and made sandcastles with the Shackleton tribe, and we went there on a play date this morning as well, which was nice. They're lovely people.'

'They are. And it was a godsend that Annie let Ed take their eight-seater car. Getting around up there wouldn't have been nearly so easy without it, but poetic justice, he and his teammate won the challenge, which was good.'

'Not your team?'

He smiled wryly. 'No. My teammate hurt her ankle, but to be honest just being so far away from the kids was enough of a challenge. It was beautiful there, though, and I'm really glad I went. Anyway, I don't want to hold you up, I expect you want to get home, don't you?'

'Don't you want me to stay tonight? If I know you, you'll want to be in early tomorrow.'

He shook his head, nothing further from his mind. 'No. Tomorrow I want to get the kids up and spend at least a little time with them before I drop them at nursery, so feel free to go, Mum. You must be exhausted. I know I am.'

She smiled gratefully. 'Oh, well, in that case...'

She kissed him goodnight and left, and he carried his luggage up, peeped round the corner at Charlie lying sprawled flat on his back across his bed, and went into Amber's room. She was snuggled on her side, but the moment he went in her eyes popped open and she scrambled up, throwing herself into his arms as he sat on the bed.

'Daddy!'

'Hello, my precious girl,' he murmured as she snuggled into him. He buried his face in her tangled hair and inhaled the smell of beach and sunshine and pasta sauce, and smiled.

It was so good to be home...

Her ankle felt better the next day.

Still sore, and she was definitely hobbling,

but whatever that crunch had been it was better rather than worse. She went to work in her trainers because they were the only shoes that fitted comfortably, and the second Sam caught sight of her she was whisked into X-Ray to get it and her ribs checked out.

'All clear,' he said, sounding relieved. 'Right, you can go home now.'

'No, I can't. I'm here to work.'

'Seriously?'

'Seriously. I'm fine.'

Sam sighed, shrugged and gave in. 'OK, but sit when you can, take breaks and put it up whenever possible. You need a bit more support on it, I think. Is that strapping adequate?'

'It's fine. It's really good. Matt knows his stuff. It feels OK.'

He rolled his eyes. 'If you say so. I'm not convinced I believe you, but we're short-staffed as usual so I'm not going to argue, but you're in Minors—and the moment it hurts—'

'Sam, I'll be fine,' she assured him, and he shrugged again and left her to it, so she went and picked up the first set of notes and found her patient, all the time wondering if Matt would be called down to the ED and if so, if he'd speak to her.

He wasn't needed, but he appeared anyway just after one, to her relief, because after the initial rush in Minors it had all settled down to a steady tick-over and she had far too much time to think about him and what her father had told her.

She was standing at the central work station filling in notes when she felt him come up behind her. How did she *know* it was him? No idea, but she did, and she turned and met his concerned eyes.

'Hi. I didn't expect you to be here,' he murmured. 'How's the ankle?'

'Better, thanks. Your strapping seems to be working. It's my mind I've got problems with. Sam's put me in Minors,' she told him, and she could hear the disgust in her voice.

So could he, evidently, because he chuckled softly.

'Yeah,' he said. 'I rang him and asked how you were, and he told me you were cross you were out of Resus.'

She laughed at that, because it was sort of true. 'I'm not really cross, and I know someone has to do Minors, but it's gone really quiet and now I'm just bored.'

'Shh, don't say that, you never say that,' he said, his eyes twinkling, and he glanced at his phone. 'Have you had lunch?'

'No. My fridge was pretty empty, and I don't

fancy chocolate or crisps out of the vending machine.'

'Well, now might be a good time to make a break for it.'

'Except I can't get to the café easily. Walking from the car park was bad enough.'

'Soon fix that,' he said, and, glancing over his shoulder, he made a satisfied noise and retrieved an abandoned wheelchair.

She stared at it in horror. 'You have to be joking.'

'Not in the slightest. Sit down or I'll put you in it.'

He would. She knew that perfectly well after yesterday, so with a sigh of resignation she sat in the wheelchair and Jenny, one of the senior nurses, nodded and grinned.

'Well done, Matt.'

'Don't encourage him—and call me if you need me, Jenny. I won't be long. And I can push myself,' she said, reaching for the wheels.

'No, you can't, it's not that sort of chair,' he pointed out, and whisked her down the corridor, out of the side entrance and into the park.

Five minutes later they were sitting on a bench under a tree, armed with cold drinks and sandwiches. He patted his lap. 'Put your leg up. I want to have a look at your ankle,' he said, and she sighed.

'If you insist,' she said, but the moment her ankle settled over that disturbingly strong thigh she could have kicked herself. She should have put it on the wheelchair, because his hands were on it and it was distracting her, and she didn't want to be distracted. She wanted to talk to him about what her father had said.

But he was probing it now, gently—or sort of gently, and she was distracted in a different way.

'Ouch!'

'Sorry. It feels swollen still. Are you sure you should be working?'

She rolled her eyes and ripped open her sandwich. 'You're as bad as Sam. You just want to fuss and cluck over me like a pair of mother hens.'

'That's why we're doctors—an exaggerated sense of responsibility for the health of the nation. It's nothing personal.'

Tell it to the fairies. His hand was resting on her leg now, his thumb idly stroking over her shin, and she wasn't even sure he was aware of doing it. She solved the problem by removing her foot from his lap and propping it on the wheelchair like she should have done in the first place, and took a deep breath.

'I spoke to my father last night and passed on your message,' she told him tentatively, 'and he asked me to send you their best wishes and said they think about you often. He spoke very fondly of you.'

'Oh, bless them. They've been amazing to me. I haven't seen them for ages, not since...'

He trailed off, but he didn't need to finish the sentence because she knew.

'He told me,' she said softly. 'About your wife. I'm so sorry. I had no idea.'

His smile was wry and a little twisted. 'I think that was rather the point. No preconceptions. No baggage. And a dead wife and two motherless little children is a lot of baggage in anyone's language.'

She winced at the frank, softly spoken words and looked away. 'I can imagine. I'm really sorry. I wish I'd known. I wouldn't have behaved like I did and I certainly wouldn't have kissed you like that. I didn't mean to offend you or overstep the mark.'

His hand reached out, his fingers finding hers. 'I wasn't in the least bit offended and you didn't overstep the mark, Livvy. There was no mark, and there was nothing wrong with your behaviour. And anyway, I kissed you first, and I shouldn't have done that, either. It was the first time I'd left the kids and gone any distance from home since—well, since then, and I just wanted to be *me*, you know? Not that poor guy whose wife died and left him with two tiny children, but just a man, someone who could be taken at face value.

'I'm sick of being different, sick of people making concessions and tiptoeing round me and worrying about upsetting me. I nearly told you, but then I realised I didn't want to because it would change everything, and I didn't *want* it to change. I was enjoying myself, having simple, uncomplicated fun with no strings, no expectations, just a man and a woman working together to achieve a series of goals and having fun on the way. And it was fun, Livvy. I wouldn't have changed any of it. Well, apart from you hurling yourself down the scree slope. That wasn't great.'

She felt her eyes fill with tears, and blinked them away, because she'd felt the same, the freedom from the burden of people's sympathy, everyone watching their words so they didn't upset or offend or reopen the emotional wounds or poke the sleeping tiger. That was why hardly anybody at the Yoxburgh Park Hospital knew her medical history, and why she hadn't told Matt.

'I wouldn't have changed any of it, either. Well, except that bit. You're right, it was fun, but I guess we're back now.'

He sighed quietly, then gave a wry huff of

laughter. 'Yes, we're back. I know that. Amber insisted on sleeping with me last night, and Charlie woke up at four, crying because he'd wet the bed, so he ended up with me as well. Definitely back. And you know what? It feels *good* to be back, and I really missed them, but I'm very, very glad I went away, too, and I'm glad you were there with me.'

She smiled at him. 'I'm glad, as well. Still, it's over now.' Odd, how that made her feel sad. Why should it? It wasn't as if anything had really happened. Just a couple of kisses, some shared banter, the odd hug. How could she miss that so much?

'It doesn't have to be over,' he said, after a long pause. 'I'd still like to see you—not in a serious way, I'm not in the market for anything more than the odd snatched lunch break or a very occasional drink or a quick bite to eat, but it would be great to have that time with you. Not that you're probably interested in such a trivial offering—'

'Of course I'm interested,' she said promptly, surprised that she was. 'I'm not in the market for anything serious, but I'm happy to spend time with you as and when we can. And I don't expect anything, Matt. I really don't.'

He nodded then, his eyes softening into a smile. 'Thank you.'

'Don't thank me. I'm relatively new here, I don't know many people yet and I have plenty of time on my hands. Spending a little of it with you will be a pleasure. And talking of time, I ought to get back, but I'm glad I've seen you so I could pass on my father's message. He spoke very highly of you, and he said your wife was a lovely person.'

A shadow crossed his eyes again, and he nodded. 'She was. Thank you. That means a lot. He was a brilliant mentor and a good friend to me, and I owe him so much. Say hi for me when you speak to him.'

'Say it yourself. I'm sure he'd love to hear from you.'

He nodded. 'Maybe I will. Right, I'd better take you back before I have Sam on the phone asking why I've abducted one of their registrars, but give me your number first.' He keyed it into his phone, and then hers jiggled in her pocket. 'Get that?'

She nodded and smiled. 'I'll send you my father's email address so you can contact him. And call me when you can, anytime you've got a gap in the chaos and you want to meet up.'

His eyes searched hers. 'It's going to be very random, Livvy. Are you sure you're OK with that?'

She nodded, although she wasn't entirely sure

what he was really offering in those random moments. Friendship? Or more? An affair? Although that might take more than the occasional coffee break, even if you were desperate.

And she wasn't that desperate, she really, really wasn't.

Was she?

CHAPTER THREE

EVEN THOUGH SHE knew he wasn't offering much or often, his 'random' turned out to be more elusive than she'd expected. Or hoped, anyway.

Maybe he'd been right to imagine that it might not be enough for her. She'd thought it would be fine, but oddly it wasn't, and even though she hardly knew him, she realised she was missing him, missing the flirting and the banter and just his presence.

By Thursday, although he'd been down to the ED at least twice that she knew of, she still hadn't seen him to speak to, but he sent her a text to ask how her ankle was, with a smiley emoji reply when she said it was better, but still nothing else. Nothing about meeting up at any time.

Sure, he'd just been away for the long week-end and was giving the children all his available time, and she knew a patient he'd seen yesterday had needed hours in Theatre because of the horrendous damage to his limbs after he'd been caught in farm machinery, and she'd seen him then, but not to speak to.

They'd instigated the major haemorrhage protocol and she'd been called in to help, but Matt, James and Sam were all there. Joe Baker, the interventional radiologist, was called down to get another line in while they tried to get control of the bleeding in their patient's limbs before he was rushed to Theatre with Matt and Joe at his side, but Matt had had no time to spare her as much as a glance. She'd heard he'd had to take the man back to Theatre today, but she hadn't heard the outcome and he might still be in there, which would explain why he hadn't contacted her.

And anyway, she kept telling herself, he was only talking about a quick coffee or the odd drink, not a relationship. And she'd managed without one for the past almost five years, so why did it suddenly matter now? She had a life. She had new friends here in Yoxburgh, old friends just thirty-five miles away in Audley, and, besides, it was the summer and if all else failed she could go for gorgeous walks along the river bank or by the sea, or get out in the front garden and weed the gravel. Goodness knows it was high time.

Which was why that evening, after a long day at work, she changed into shorts and trainers and a tatty old T-shirt and tackled it. If nothing else it would distract her from a man who was clearly far too busy to fit her into his chaotic life, and it certainly wasn't a moment too soon because the little bit of garden behind the hedge was a mess.

The weeds had flourished in the glorious early summer weather, rooting themselves firmly down in the supposedly low-maintenance gravel, and she was wrestling with a particularly stubborn weed when she heard footsteps approaching.

'Oh, get *out*!' she growled, and the footsteps stopped.

'Well, that's a warm welcome.'

She jackknifed up, lost her balance and stepped back without thinking, and pain shot through her ankle. Her leg folded as she yelped, and he caught her and took the weight off it, holding her firmly back against his chest.

'Are you OK?'

She straightened up and turned to face him, carefully this time, her heart thudding a little as she met his eyes. 'Yes, I'm fine or I was, until you made me jump.'

He stifled the smile. 'Sorry. Here, let me,' he said, and taking the little fork out of her hand, he shoved it into the ground beside the weed, levered gently and lifted it out, its roots intact.

'There you go. One late weed. Am I forgiven?'

'Only if you take the rest of them out.'

He humphed and lobbed it into the garden waste bin.

'So, what brings you here?' she asked, cursing the fact that she was hot, sweaty, covered in dirt and quite definitely not at her fragrant best. 'I'm sure it wasn't my weeds, although don't let me stop you.'

He chuckled. 'No, not your weeds. I tried to ring you, but you didn't answer, so I thought I'd call by, just in case.'

Her heart skipped a beat. 'Just in case?'

He smiled. 'In case you were in and had a few minutes to spare.'

She looked down at herself. Yes, she had time to spare, but... 'I can't go anywhere, Matt. Look at me!'

His eyes tracked over her. 'I am,' he said, his voice warm. 'And I wasn't planning on going anywhere. I just thought it might be nice to have a coffee with you here, if you can drag yourself away from the weeds for a few minutes?'

Drag herself away? Wouldn't take much dragging. 'Sure. Come on in.'

She picked up her tools and gloves and led him back inside along the hall, through the dining area and into the kitchen.

'You're still limping. I hope that's not my fault.'

It was, because he'd made her jump, but she wasn't going to tell him that. 'I said it was better, I didn't say it was cured. Coffee?'

She turned but he was right behind her, his hands coming up to steady her as she winced again and shifted her weight off her sore ankle.

'Steady,' he murmured, and she could feel the warmth of his hands cupping her shoulders, the cool drift of his minty-fresh breath, and their eyes locked.

Was he going to kiss her? Please…

No. He dropped his hands, took a step back and looked away, and she swallowed her disappointment.

'Um—yes, please, white coffee, no sugar.'

She washed her hands, put the kettle on and opened the cupboard, and he settled himself on a dining chair and looked around.

'It'll have to be decaf, I'm afraid,' she told him.

'That's fine, whatever you've got. I've had quite a lot today, anyway. It's been a tough day.'

'Really? What happened?'

He sighed and scrubbed a hand through his hair. 'We lost the farmer. I'd taken him back to Theatre twice to try and salvage what I could of his limbs, but he'd lost so much blood so quickly before they could get him out that his brain was deprived of oxygen and today his organs shut down and we turned off the life support.'

She stopped, spoon in hand. 'Oh, no. Oh, Matt, I'm really sorry to hear that. Did he have a wife?'

'Yes, and three children. Telling her was— well, I think she was expecting it, but even so. He was only thirty-six. Same age as me. That was tough.'

It must have been, especially having once been on the receiving end himself, but she imagined that would give him a better understanding of the impact of it. Would that make it easier, or harder?

'Nice house, by the way,' he said as she poured water onto the coffee. 'How long have you been here?'

'Since I took over from Iona Baker's locum when she handed in her notice after her maternity leave. I was working in London but I wanted to come home to Suffolk, and the job came up so I took it, and Sam put me in touch with Ben Walker, one of the obstetricians. It belongs to his wife and I moved in in April but unfortunately I'm only renting it. I gather they only let it to hospital staff.'

'Yes, Ed said he lived here for a while before his grandfather died. It's interesting.'

It was. It had started life as a typical Victorian semi, but the dining room had been opened to the hall and the kitchen, and a door led out via a conservatory to the back garden, so the whole room felt light and airy.

It wasn't everyone's taste, but she loved it.

'It is interesting, isn't it? It's a pity Daisy won't sell. I sold my flat in London and I'm waiting for it all to go through, then I'm going to buy something, but I'm not sure where. Maybe here, maybe Audley, although if I want to go home I can always stay with my parents so I'm a bit undecided, but there's no rush. I love this house and I'm quite happy here for now.'

And then the conversation died, leaving them standing there in a slightly awkward silence while his coffee brewed and her green tea steamed gently beside it.

'Matt…'

'Livvy…'

He laughed softly and gestured to her. 'You first.'

'I was going to ask you why you wanted to see me.'

He frowned slightly. 'I told you—I thought we could have a coffee.'

'No. I meant—generally. Why you wanted to make time to do this.'

His frown deepened, his eyes concerned and a little confused. 'I thought we had this conversation on Monday?'

'We did, but—I'm not really sure I know what you want from me. I've spent days trying to work it out, and I'm still not convinced I know the answer. It could be so many things. Friendship, an affair, friends with benefits—?'

'Friends with benefits?'

He stood up and walked over to her, stopping just inches away, hands rammed in his back pockets, a quizzical look in his eyes, and she shrugged helplessly.

'Well, I don't know—I told you I can't work it out.'

His soft laugh rippled over her and made her skin tingle. 'Oh, Livvy. There's nothing to work out. I don't *want* anything from you, I just thought it would be nice to spend time together. And I think we both know it's probably more than simple friendship, but if that's all you want to offer me, I'll happily accept it, and there's no hurry. I just want to see you. I feel we hardly scratched the surface over the weekend, and there's so much more to you that I don't know, and I want to know more. I want to spend time with you, just be with you and hang out. No agenda. No pressure. Just see where it goes.'

He looked down at the floor, then up again, his eyes sombre now as he spoke again, his voice low.

'I can't offer you a relationship, not one I can do justice to, but I'm lonely, Livvy. I'm ridiculously busy, constantly surrounded by people, and I'm hardly ever alone, and yet I'm lonely. I miss the companionship of a woman, and I'd like to spend time with one who isn't either simply a colleague or my mother. A woman who can make me laugh again. I spend my days rushed off my feet, the rest of my time is dedicated to my children, and don't get me wrong, I love them desperately, but—I have no downtime, no me-time, no time to chill out and have a conversation about something that isn't medicine or hospital politics or whether the kids want dippy eggs or scrambled.'

His mouth kicked up in a wry smile, and he shrugged, just a subtle shift of his shoulders that was more revealing than even his words had been, and she forgot the coffee, forgot her foot and her common sense, and walked up to him, put her arms round him and hugged him.

'Scrambled, every time,' she said, her voice slightly choked, and it took a second, but then he laughed, his chest shaking under her ear, and he tilted her head back and kissed her. Just briefly, not long enough to cause trouble, just long enough to remind her of what he did to her, and then he rested his forehead against her and smiled.

'Me, too. Preferably with bacon and slices of cold tomato in a massive club sandwich washed down with a bucket of coffee.'

'Oh, yes! I haven't had one of those for ages!'

He laughed and let her go. 'I'll cook you brunch one day,' he said, and it sounded like a promise.

'Is that a promise?' she asked, just to be sure. 'Not that I'll hold you to it, and I'm not in a position to do a relationship justice either for various reasons—work, health...'

'Health?'

She shrugged, not yet ready to tell him, to throw *that* word into the middle of a casual conversation. 'Amongst other things, but—whatever you want from me, wherever you want to take this, I'm up for it.'

'Is that what you want from this? An ad hoc affair?'

She held his eyes, wondering if she dared, if she had the courage to tell him, to let him that close, to open herself to potential hurt. Because she'd have to, if this was going any further.

But there was nothing in his eyes except need and tenderness, and she knew he wouldn't hurt her. She nodded. 'Yes. Yes, it is, if that's what you want, too.'

His breath huffed out, a quiet, surprised sound, and something flared in his eyes. 'Oh, Livvy. Absolutely. As long as we're on the same page.'

'We're on the same page,' she said, and he nodded slowly and dipped his head, taking her mouth in a lingering, tender kiss. And then he straightened, just as it was hotting up, and stepped away with a wry smile.

'Is that coffee ready? I don't have very long and certainly not long enough for where that was going. I begged yet another favour from my sainted mother and I don't want to take her for granted.'

She nodded and turned back to pour it with shaking hands, then felt his fingers curl over her shoulders as he moved in behind her and rested his head against the side of hers, doing all sorts of things to her heart rate.

'That's yes to brunch, by the way,' he murmured, his voice deep and husky. 'It *is* a promise. Goodness knows when, but soon.'

Heat raced through her, and she pressed the plunger down, filled his mug and handed it to him with a shaky smile.

'Here. Shall we go in the back garden? It's a bit of a jungle but it's such a lovely evening.'

'Sure. I love a jungle and it'll make a refreshing change from mine. It's hardly got a stick in it.'

She led him through the conservatory and they sat on the swinging bench at the end in the dappled shade under the wisteria, wrapped around by the whisper of a light sea breeze through the leaves and the quiet creak of the chains as he rocked the bench with a little thrust of his foot, and he sighed.

'This is lovely—it reminds me of the garden we had in London, cool and green and shady. So tranquil, like a little oasis in the madness.'

'It is. It's my favourite place. Work's so busy, and here I can just chill out and be me.'

He nodded. 'I know just what you mean. My current garden was wildly overgrown so I had it landscaped over the winter, but until the trees and shrubs grow back and the beds fill out it just looks barren, and I hate it.'

'It'll grow,' she said encouragingly, and he smiled.

'I know. I'm just impatient, and I really miss our London garden. It became my sanctuary, and when we moved I lost that place where I could go and find solitude. The nearest I get to it now is on the balcony and that's not exactly private, but I've pretty much given up on that. The only place I ever get any privacy is in the bathroom, and that's only if I lock the door, and unless they're asleep the chances of one of the children banging on it and demanding my attention are super-high.'

His mouth tipped up in a wry smile, and she laughed.

'Are they that bad?'

He shook his head. 'No. They're lovely, but they're just always *there*. Don't get me wrong, I love them to bits and I couldn't bear it if anything happened to them, but sometimes I just want to run away and hide.'

She searched his eyes, finding humour but also a little despair. 'Feel free to come here whenever you want,' she said softly. 'You're always welcome to join me. Or I can give you a key and you can let yourself in.'

He smiled, just a slow, slight tilt of his mouth, and then he lifted his coffee to his lips and took a long swallow. 'Thank you.'

'Any time. So, tell me about your children— or are they off limits?'

He smiled a tender, slightly rueful smile and tensed his thigh, giving the swing another push and making the chains creak again. 'No, they're not off limits,' he said fondly. 'Amber starts school in September and she's massively excited and more than ready for it, and Charlie—well, Charlie's just a little boy. He's either running or he's asleep but I expect he might grow out of that. He's not three till August.'

She felt her eyes well. 'It must be so tough being a single parent. How do you cope? How *did* you cope?'

'I don't know. I don't think I did, really. When Juliet died—' He broke off, then gave her a crooked smile. 'It was tough. It's still tough, but it's getting easier, and my mother's been amazing and so have Juliet's parents and her sister, Sally. Without them I couldn't do it, which is why I took the job up here, because Sally's only ten miles away, her parents are a little further, and my mother lives literally round the corner from my house. And I've got friends here. Ed and I go back years, but still... Don't get me wrong, it's a great job and I love it, but it's not where I was heading.'

'No, my father said that. I think he'd imagined you heading up a major trauma centre.'

He smiled wryly. 'Yeah, me, too, but it's not really compatible with family life, or at least not on the way there. Maybe once I'd made it. And maybe that's the only good thing to have come out of this, that I've found a job with virtually no commuting time, that gives the children regular, meaningful contact with other members of the family and me enough job satisfaction that I don't feel in the slightest bit cheated. Well, maybe a bit, professionally, but that's a small sacrifice and nothing compared to what we all gain as a family from us being here, and frankly there have been times when I wasn't even sure we'd all make it through.'

Oh, Matt…

He glanced at his watch and swore softly. 'I need to go. I'm sorry.'

'Don't be,' she murmured, her heart aching for him. 'It's been lovely to see you. I'm glad you came.'

His mouth kicked up into another crooked grin. 'Me, too. I'm still sorry it can't be longer, though,' he added, and the slight disappointment she'd felt at his short visit faded away.

'It's fine, Matt. I understand. And remember, you can come here at any time.'

'Thank you. For that, for understanding, and for the coffee. It means a lot.' He got to his feet, setting the swing rocking gently. 'Don't move, I'll let myself out. You stay there and enjoy the last of the evening sun.'

He leant over, his hand cradling her cheek, and touched his lips to hers in a tender, lingering kiss that wasn't nearly long enough. Then he was gone, leaving her mulling over his words.

There have been times when I wasn't even sure we'd all make it through...

How on earth had he coped? How had the children coped? Poor, tiny little things. She thought of her parents, of how much they loved each other, how close they all were as a family, and then she imagined one or other of them dying and their whole world being torn apart.

Something wet landed on her arm, and it took her a moment to realise that it was a tear. She scrubbed it away, sucked in a deep breath and headed back to the front garden. A bit of hard physical work was just what she needed, and her ankle would just have to get over itself.

She didn't see him again until the following week, and when she did they hardly had time to acknowledge each other because by the time he came down to the ED she was assisting James Slater as he opened the chest of a teenager with stab wounds.

'Perfect timing,' James said bluntly, and she heard the snap of gloves and then Matt was there, gently shouldering her out of the way and taking over, his hands finding the bleed instantly.

'OK, the pulmonary vein's been nicked and this lobe is trashed. Can I have a clamp and some more suction, please?'

She'd seen him in action before but not like this, wrist deep inside the chest of a dying boy—except the boy didn't die, because he stopped the bleed, and found another and stopped that, too, and then turned his attention to the other wounds in his abdomen.

'He needs opening up. Has anyone had time to look at his back?'

'Yes, it's clear,' James said, and he nodded.

'Right, I need to transfer him to Theatre. Can someone alert them, please?'

'Done it, and I've got PICU on standby,' a nurse said.

'*PICU?* How old is he?' he asked, sounding startled.

'Fifteen,' James growled.

Matt swore softly under his breath and stepped back from the bed. 'OK, let's pack that and get a sterile dressing over it for the transfer, and then we'll see how it goes.'

Once he was satisfied the boy was ready to go he stepped back and stripped off his gloves and the blood-splattered plastic apron, turning towards the door and meeting her eyes for the first time. His face softened briefly into a smile that barely reached his eyes.

'Hi. Thanks for your help. Sorry, I'm a bit rushed. I'll catch up with you later. Right, let's go.'

All business again, he headed out of the door, one hand on the trolley, and James thanked her and sent her back to the patient she'd left when the boy had been brought in. She picked up where she'd left off, but her mind kept straying to Matt and the boy he was trying to save.

Would he be able to? Would the poor kid make it through?

Please, please don't let him die...

He didn't die, to Matt's surprise.

He almost did. He had a couple of goes in Theatre and they'd had to restart his heart once, but now he was in PICU, still critical but at least with a fighting chance of being more than another tragic statistic.

He left the hospital late after he'd talked to Ryan's desperate mother and went home to his children, gathering them up in a massive cuddle on the sofa, blinking hard to shift the tears that welled unexpectedly in his eyes.

'Tough day?' his mother asked, and he gave a grunt of humourless laughter.

'You could say that. It could have been worse, though.'

She nodded, as if she'd understood the subtext. 'I'll make you a cup of tea.'

'Decaf, please. And can you stay? I might need to go back in.'

'Yes, darling, of course I can.'

He sighed, let go of the children, who were squirming in his arms and trying to watch the television, and followed his mother into the kitchen area.

'I don't know what I'd do without you,' he mumbled, and wrapped his arms around her from behind, resting his head against hers. 'You've been a star, Mum.'

'No, I've been a parent. That's what we do, Matt, that's what families are for. We pick up the pieces. You know that.'

'I do, but you've had more than your fair share of it.'

She shrugged, her shoulders shifting against his chest, and the kettle clicked off and he dropped his arms and let her make the tea.

It was only four years since his father had died, and she'd been amazing, nursing him through the final stages of cancer with humour and compassion, and when he'd gone she'd picked up the pieces of her life and carried on, and then, two years later, she'd put her own grief aside and picked up the pieces of *his* life and his children's when Jules had died and left them all devastated.

So soon after losing her husband, that must have been incredibly tough for her, but she'd done it without question, dropped everything and come to him.

Foolishly he'd refused to take any time off work, so after the funeral he'd put the children in nursery and sent his mother home, but they'd been too distraught so after three days she'd come back to look after them in the family home, but that had meant he was never alone so he was bottling up his grief, snapping at everyone and shutting down his emotions because he was afraid of what would happen if he let go.

So after a few more days she'd brought them back up here because he thought it would be better for them to have a calm, orderly life, with him appearing every weekend pleased to see them, rather than be in their own home with him coming back in the evenings crabby and angry and needing to fall apart.

He'd taken time off then, a couple of weeks when he'd hardly got out of bed, just lain in the sheets that still smelt of Jules and cried until his chest ached and his eyes were raw and his heart felt as if it had been torn in two.

But they'd missed him desperately, and he'd missed them, too, so he'd finally pulled himself together and changed the sheets, cleaned the house and his mother had brought the children back to London and stayed, and when the job in Yoxburgh had come up, she'd helped him get the house ready to put on the market, shown the buyers round it and packed up all their things for storage until the new house was ready.

All except Juliet's things.

He'd done that, working on autopilot, and he hadn't dealt with them until the week before he'd gone to Cumbria. Now they were packed in boxes in his study, ready for the children to look at when they were old enough.

He hadn't felt ready until then, just as he now wasn't ready for what he felt with Livvy, either, but it seemed to be happening, some slow awakening of his senses, a thawing of a part of him that had been numb for two years.

Was it wise? Probably not.

Disloyal?

No, not that. Jules wouldn't have wanted him to be lonely, but he still had unfinished business with her. If only he'd had time to say goodbye, but by the time he'd got to the hospital she had been in a coma and it had been too late.

Had she known he was there? He hoped so, hoped she'd known how much he loved her, how much she'd given him over the years, how much he had to thank her for—

'Matt?'

He blinked, his eyes coming back into focus, and took the tea from his mother. 'Thanks,' he said gruffly. 'Sorry, I was miles away.'

'I know,' she said, her eyes so full of compassion and understanding it nearly unravelled him. 'Come on, let's sit down with the children for a few minutes until their film finishes and then you can put them to bed—unless you'd like me to do it?'

He shook his head. 'No. I'll do it. Oh, damn. Don't you have book club tonight?'

She smiled ruefully. 'I do, but it doesn't matter. I haven't finished the book.'

'Do you ever?'

She laughed. 'Sometimes.'

'Go anyway. I'm sure it doesn't matter. Where is it?'

'Only round the corner. Joanna's house— Annie's mother, and Marnie will be there, too. Maybe I will go, if you're sure you're all right?'

'I'm fine, Mum. You're only seconds away, so I'll call you if I need to go back in.'

'That wasn't what I meant,' she said, and he had to look away. He cleared his throat.

'So, what have they had to eat? Let me guess—pasta.'

'No. Actually, no, for once. I made them a chicken tagine with couscous. They loved it. I've saved you some, but you'll probably think it's a bit mild.'

'I'm sure it'll be lovely. I'm starving. Thank you—for everything.'

His mother flapped her hand at him and headed back to the sofa with her tea, and he followed her, sat down on the other sofa and watched the end of the programme with his precious children snuggled up on each side of him while his tea cooled, forgotten.

Livvy saw him on Monday in Resus, over a week since he'd come to her house, and they went for coffee after his patient was transferred to Interventional Radiology with Joe Baker and he was off the hook for a few minutes.

She'd been on edge since their conversation that Thursday and for some reason the time had seemed to stretch interminably, so she was ridiculously pleased when he asked her to join him. Maybe he'd take the opportunity to arrange a time to see her properly, when they could be alone.

He picked up a banana, asked for a cappuccino and Livvy ordered a pot of green tea and found a bag of mixed nuts and seeds, her heart jiggling in her chest.

Would he suggest it?

'Do you ever drink coffee?' he asked as they sat down, and she shook her head.

'Not usually. I'm not a huge fan.'

'But—green tea?' he asked, pulling a face. 'Is that for health reasons?'

Again, not the right time, and not enough time to discuss it properly, but it settled her heart down again. 'Partly. It's good for you,' she said, without going into any further details. 'And anyway, I love it.'

He laughed. 'I can't imagine why. I think it's vile, but each to his own. I emailed your father, by the way,' he added. 'I've been meaning to contact him for ages and I've never got round to it, so thanks for jogging me. Anyway, he replied and said it would be nice to see me again, so I might run up there sometime if I get a minute. I could maybe take the children one weekend.'

She nodded. 'They'd love that, but don't plan it for this coming weekend. It's Dad's sixtieth, and they're throwing him a party on Saturday night. Actually,' she said, thinking about it and wondering if it would provide that opportunity she was waiting for, 'you ought to come with me.'

He shook his head. 'No, I can't do that.'

She felt a little stab of disappointment. 'Oh. I suppose you'd have to get someone to look after the children and it's very short notice. That's a shame.'

He shook his head again. 'I wouldn't, as it happens, because they're having a sleepover with their cousins at Juliet's sister's house, but there's the small matter that I haven't been invited.'

'Yes, you have—by me,' she said, taking away that excuse with a smile. 'You can be my plus one. I'll even drive you so you can drink—unless you don't want to come?' she added, suddenly wondering if she'd overstepped the mark. Again.

'Won't you be staying over?'

She shook her head. 'I don't have to. I was going to, but I'm sure they can use my room for someone else. Seriously, Matt, why not? It'll be a great party. Unless you're working?'

'No. No, I'm not working, but it just feels a bit cheeky.'

'Rubbish, you'd be more than welcome.'

He frowned, but he didn't say any more, just glanced at his phone and sighed. 'I need to go. I've got a patient to check on and then I've got an outpatients' clinic.'

'Yeah, I should go, too. But please think

about it. I'm sure they'd be delighted if you came. I know they'd love to see you.'

And she'd love him to come, if she could only persuade him...

He laughed, his eyes creasing. 'You don't give up, do you?'

She smiled wryly. 'No, but just tell me this. If he'd asked you himself, would you have said yes?'

'Probably. Well, after I'd talked to you and made sure you were OK with it.'

She laughed. 'Why wouldn't I be OK with it?'

'I don't know, but it doesn't do to make assumptions,' he said softly, surprising her.

'Matt, you should know me better by now,' she scolded gently. 'I'm more than happy if you want to come. Think about it and let me know.'

He nodded. 'OK. And that's not a yes, by the way.'

'Of course it isn't,' she said, but she couldn't stop her smile and he rolled his eyes, laughed and walked her back to the ED.

CHAPTER FOUR

HE DIDN'T GET a minute to see her in the next few days, but her invitation was never far from his mind and he still didn't know what to do about it.

He hadn't been to a party since Jules had died, mostly because he hadn't had the time or the inclination, but this was Oliver's sixtieth, a milestone party for a man to whom he owed so much, for all sorts of reasons. Did he want to go with Livvy?

Yes, he realised. He did—but was it wise? Their relationship was so new, so unformed that he wasn't even sure they *had* one. Their only conversation about it had ended with talk of an ad hoc affair, and he certainly wasn't ready to go public with that, especially not with her parents, of all people.

Except, of course, because it was so new, they probably wouldn't think anything of it other than that their daughter was his colleague and so it was entirely reasonable that they should go to the party together. They didn't need to announce to anyone that they were starting a relationship—if you could call something so hit and miss a relationship.

She didn't seem to want more than that, though, which was fine by him because he couldn't give her more anyway, but one of the reasons she'd given was health issues, and that intrigued him. What health issues? She hadn't said, and he hadn't seen her in the sort of situation when he felt he could ask. Maybe on the way to the party, or the way back?

And the party was a way of getting to see Bron and Oliver again, a way to thank Oliver personally for what he'd done for him, but also a chance to see more of Livvy, and spend more than fifteen snatched minutes with her over a cup of green tea, for heaven's sake!

He sent her a text.

Is the invitation still open?

Seconds later her reply pinged back.

Yes, of course. It's black tie—is that a problem?

No problem. What time shall I pick you up?

It starts at seven thirty. And I'm driving. I'll pick you up.

He laughed. Yes, she'd offered, but he wouldn't hold her to it. For a start it just felt wrong, and more importantly he never went anywhere without being able to get away under his own steam—just in case. Except Cumbria, and he would have hired a car or caught a train or got a taxi if necessary. And that was exceptional. Audley was about thirty miles up the road, less than an hour away. And he didn't need alcohol. He'd had enough to last a lifetime in that lonely fortnight after Jules had died, and he was fine without it.

Besides, if he was with her and she was dancing in some slinky little number that was going to trash his mind, he needed to be stone-cold sober or he might well make an idiot of himself in front of her parents.

I'll drive you. Call me old-fashioned. :)

There was a pause—a long one. Because she was busy? Quite likely. It was half an hour before she came back to him.

Not going to argue. I hate driving at night! Pick me up at six forty-five. X

He was late.

Only a couple of minutes, but it was enough to stretch her tight nerves just a little tighter.

She'd been ready ages ago, dithering over whether her new dress was all right, if he'd like it, if she should wear her hair up or down, could she wear heels—only low ones but still, her ankle wasn't quite right yet—and how much make-up? She hardly wore any usually, but tonight—

And the dress. She'd loved the dress the moment she'd seen it, and it could have been made for her. The left shoulder was bare, with diagonal pleats across the bodice that started at the waist and ran up to the right shoulder, ending in a delicate waterfall of chiffon like a floaty little cap sleeve that covered the top of her arm. It was pretty, elegant, fitted her like a glove and was a perfect match for her eyes, but she'd spent the last few years hiding herself away in loose, casual clothes and it was—well, fitted, for want of a better word. And dressy.

She'd told herself off for being ridiculous. It was beautifully cut, and it was a glamorous party, so why shouldn't she be dressy? So she'd twisted her hair up and secured it with a sparkly clip, put on her normal going-out make-up and the wedge-heeled sandals and gone downstairs to wait, her nerves as tight as a bowstring because tonight might be the night, and she felt like a teenager going to her first prom.

She was watching from the bay window of her little sitting room when he arrived, and as he rounded the front of the car and stepped onto the kerb, she felt her mouth dry.

What was it about formal dress that made men look so good? Not that Matt didn't always, but tonight he looked stunning as he strode up the path and waved to her through the window. Even sexier, if that was possible, and her pulse hitched.

She hesitated at the front door, ran a hand over her dress, wondering again if he'd like it, hoping he would, telling herself it didn't matter when she knew it did, then finally she opened the door, and he smiled again as he stepped inside and dropped a kiss on her cheek, his eyes warm.

'You look amazing,' he said, his voice low and soft and a little rough at the same time, and she felt the tension ease a little. Well, no, that tension. The other tension, the tension that was all about how gorgeous he looked and how much she was looking forward to spending all that time with him on a—was it a date?—ratcheting up a notch or six.

'Well, I thought I'd lash out on a new dress,'

she said, her voice oddly breathless. 'He's only going to be sixty once.'

His voice deepened a fraction and his eyes never left her face. 'I wasn't talking about the dress.' Then his eyes dropped, and he scanned her slowly and smiled. 'Although I have to say it really suits you. You look beautiful, Livvy. Absolutely gorgeous. He'll be so proud of you.'

She felt soft colour sweeping up her throat, and felt suddenly shy. She was never shy! What was he doing to her?

'Thank you,' she said, fighting down the unexpected blush and scanning him blatantly just for the fun of it. 'You don't look so bad yourself.'

He grinned. 'That's because you're used to seeing me in scrubs. It's just the tux. Same old me underneath, I'm afraid.'

'Yeah, that must be it, all in the tailoring,' she said, making a joke of it while she dragged her tattered composure back into shape and tried not to think about what was underneath the immaculately cut suit. She picked up her bag and a soft cashmere wrap in case it was cold later, and turned back to him.

'Shall we go?'

He gestured to the front door and gave a little mock bow. 'Your carriage awaits. I even washed it.'

'Good grief. That's going above and beyond.'

He chuckled and opened the car door for her and helped her in, lifting her dress clear of the sill so it didn't get dirty, even though the car was gleaming.

So thoughtful. So—perfect? And so unavailable...

No. Not unavailable. Just not permanent. There was a difference, and she was looking forward to exploring it.

'I take it you know the way to their house?' she asked as he slid behind the wheel, and he laughed softly.

'Yes, I know the way. Sit back and relax.'

Livvy walked through the open front door of the Victorian house on the park that was her family home, and Matt followed her in, hanging back a little.

Her father was there greeting his guests, and he looked fit and well and nothing like sixty. He hadn't changed, not in the two years since he'd seen him, and very little in the nine years since he'd first joined Oliver's team as a baby registrar, and he saw the love in his eyes as he pulled his daughter into a hug and kissed her cheek.

'Hello, darling. You look beautiful,' he said

warmly, and then he looked up and his eyes widened.

'Matt! Come in! How good to see you!'

'You, too. Happy birthday,' he said, holding out the bottle of champagne he'd brought him, and Oliver thanked him and took it, then wrapped him firmly in a hug that spoke volumes before he dropped his arms and stepped back, his eyes warm and filled with compassion. 'Oh, it's so good to see you again. Livvy said she was bringing someone, but she wouldn't say who, and I'm so glad it's you. It's been much too long,' Oliver said warmly, then slung an arm around his shoulders and wheeled him down the hall. 'Come and see Bron, she's in the kitchen. Bron, look who Livvy's brought!'

Her eyes lit up. 'Matt!' She set down the tray of canapés, wiped her hands and enveloped him in a hug. 'Oh, Matt, it's *so* good to see you again. I'm so—' She broke off, hugged him harder and let go, her eyes suddenly over-bright. 'How are you? How are the children?'

'We're fine,' he said firmly. 'Really. They're growing up fast. Amber starts school in September, and she's well and truly ready for it, and Charlie—well, Charlie's just exhausting. My poor mother's run ragged, but she loves them to bits and they love her, and—you know, we're getting by. Still, I'm not here to talk about me, I want to hear all about you two, but I guess you're busy.'

She laughed. 'Just a little, but there are lots of people you'll know. Here, grab a tray of canapés, wander out into the garden and pass them round and find yourself a drink and I'll catch up with you later. I want to see pictures of the children.'

He chuckled, took the tray from her and headed out to the garden as instructed. There was a marquee in the middle of the lawn and it was teeming with people, some of whom he'd worked with. Ross Hamilton was there, one of the general surgeons and a contemporary of Oliver's, talking to Jack Lawrence, the ED clinical lead. They would have heard about Jules, and he wondered if they'd feel they had to say something, or if they'd just avoid him. He'd had a lot of that and he suddenly wished he hadn't come—

A hand slipped into the crook of his arm with a little squeeze. 'Sorry, I got caught by some old friends and I've been looking for you everywhere—where did you go?'

He looked down at her with a smile, glad that she was back by his side, noticing how the cornflower blue of her eyes seemed to be made even brighter by the dress, which matched them exactly. The dress that was playing hell with his blood pressure. The dress he wanted to peel slowly off her and—

'Your father took me into the kitchen to see your mother, and she handed me this tray of canapés and put me to work.'

'Typical.' Livvy laughed up at him, and he felt as if the sun had come out. 'So, who do you remember, and who do you recognise and can't place?'

He smiled but he could feel it was a little crooked. 'To be honest, I'm happy just hanging out with you, Livvy. I've hardly seen you for days—'

'Matt!'

He turned to find Ross and Lizzi Hamilton had come up behind him. He'd met Lizzi several times, and the first thing she did was hug him wordlessly.

'Good to see you,' Ross said, his voice a little rough as his hand engulfed Matt's and shook it firmly. 'So, how are things? I gather from Oliver that you're working with Livvy in Yoxburgh?'

'Not with her, but she's a trauma doctor so we meet in Resus pretty often.' Not often enough, if he was honest, but it was better than nothing, which seemed to be the alternative.

They chatted for a bit while he force-fed

them canapés, then they moved on and he turned to Livvy. 'I need a drink, I haven't got one yet and I could murder a glass of something cold and wet and alcohol-free.'

'Come.' She slipped her hand through his arm and led him into the huge conservatory where a bar had been set up, and took the tray of canapés from him to put it down by the glasses. 'So, what do you fancy? Fizzy water? Cola, tonic, juice, elderflower cordial, a fruit punch—guaranteed non-alcoholic? Or there might be some alcohol-free beer.'

'That sounds good.'

She whipped the top off a bottle and handed it to him, picked up a glass of sparkling water, put a handful of the canapés in a paper napkin and steered him back down the garden to a vacant bench tucked under the eaves of the old coach house. A glorious fragrant rose smothered the red-brick wall, and the delicate scent surrounded them as they sat down.

Livvy sighed. 'Oh, that's better. I should have realised it was too soon to wear heels,' she grumbled softly, and he rolled his eyes and sighed and took one of the canapés.

'You don't say. What are you trying to do— twist it again?'

'All right, all right, I know it's stupid, but

they're only low wedges and I wanted to look nice.'

'Nice?' He laughed under his breath, and shook his head at her. 'Livvy, you couldn't fail to look nice, especially in that dress. And you look more than nice. Much, much more.'

He felt his smile fade, driven out by something unexpectedly powerful, and he could see an echo of it in her eyes, an unfulfilled yearning, a need that hadn't been met. Yet.

Not now!

He looked away quickly and turned his attention back to the colourful and glamorous crowd.

'It's a good turn-out.'

'It is. I'm glad. They've got dancing later in the marquee.'

He felt his heart thud. 'Will you be able to dance?'

She laughed. 'If I take my shoes off, and anyway, I'll have you to hold me up. I'm not going to be jiving.'

'Well, not with me, anyway. I draw the line at making a total fool of myself but don't worry, I won't stand on you and I will hold you up.' Although it might kill him to hold her that close...

'Good,' she said, and then she slipped off

her shoes, scooped them up and got to her feet again.

'Come on, my brother and sister are here and they want to see you again.'

'Hold on, let me remember their names. Is it Jamie?'

'Yes, and my little sister's Abbie. Did you know she had a crush on you?'

He groaned and rolled his eyes. 'Seriously?'

She laughed up at him, her eyes sparkling, and he had a desperate need to kiss her. He stifled it fast.

'Seriously,' she was saying. 'She was only sixteen then. I'm sure she's outgrown it. She's twenty-five now, lives with her boyfriend and she's a doctor.'

'It seems to run in the family.'

'No, Jamie broke the mould. He's an architect. Here they are. Hi, guys. Remember Matt?'

The group parted to let them in, and he smiled and shook hands and then contented himself with watching Livvy.

It was no hardship.

They chatted until the music started, and then he and Livvy ended up on the dance floor. Her ankle was giving her a bit of grief, so he held her, as promised, and the feel of her in his arms and against his body trashed his last shreds of detachment. He didn't care who saw them together, what they thought—didn't care about any of it.

All he cared about was holding her, but the music stopped at midnight, hauling him back to reality, and they ended up in the kitchen, clustered round the table, with just the family left.

Jackets had been abandoned long ago, bow ties were hanging, top buttons and cufflinks well and truly undone, and with everyone else gone he could finally relax.

He was sitting beside Livvy at the table, and Bron was busy with the kettle while Oliver piled the last of the canapés onto a plate and put them on the table next to a cheeseboard.

'Coffee, Matt?'

'Oh, please, Bron, nice and strong. I need something to keep me awake. I'm too old for this malarkey.'

'I don't know, the young have no stamina,' Oliver said, rolling his eyes.

'Maybe we've just had less champagne,' Abbie said drily, and everyone laughed.

Bron put the coffee down in front of Matt, and Oliver caught her and pulled her onto his lap. 'That was a great party, darling. Thank you,' he said lovingly, and kissed her.

'Oh, yuck, get a room,' Jamie heckled, laughing, and Oliver joined in the laughter.

'It's my birthday' he said, 'and I'll kiss my wife if I want to.'

'Quite right,' Livvy said. 'You ignore him, Dad.'

'So, Livvy,' Bron said, settling back against Oliver's shoulder and looking perfectly content, 'tell us all about this trip to Cumbria.'

'Oh, it was great—well, right up until I hurt my ankle.'

'Yes, how *did* you do that?' Abbie asked, and Matt snorted and everyone's eyes swivelled to him.

'What?' Abbie asked.

He shrugged. 'Ask her,' he said, unable to stifle the smile, and then he caught her eye and they both started to laugh.

'What?' Abbie said again, joining in the laughter, and he shrugged again.

'Oh, it was silly, really. She was nagging me for not going fast enough, worried we weren't going to be first to the top, and I told her to be careful because the path was unstable, and she said, "I'm always careful", and then it crumbled and she fell down a scree slope. Luckily she hit a rock.'

'*Luckily?*' Oliver said, frowning at her in

concern. 'You never said anything about a rock, Livvy.'

'That doesn't surprise me,' he said drily. 'It was about forty or fifty feet down, right at the top of the slope, really. If it hadn't stopped her…' He felt his smile fade. 'Well, it was a long way to the bottom, put it like that, and the rock broke her fall and fortunately nothing else.'

His laughter was long gone, driven out by the remembered horror, his fear that she was dead, his relief when she started to breathe again.

'She was badly winded, but that was all. That and a few colourful bruises and the ankle, of course, but I didn't know that at the time so it was a bit worrying. She was very lucky. And she was all for us going on up and her making her own way down when she couldn't put any weight on it and could have cracked a rib and got a pneumothorax or a ruptured spleen or—'

'I don't have one any more.'

'Yeah, but I didn't know that at the time, and you still have lungs.'

'Anyway, I knew I was all right.'

'Yeah, of course you did, because you have X-ray eyes,' he said drily. 'So, needless to say, I ignored her and took her down, protesting all the way, but that's Livvy, I guess, she just won't give up fighting. More guts than sense.'

'Oh, we know all about that,' Oliver said softly, his eyes flicking to Livvy, and she laughed and changed the subject abruptly, as if she was suddenly uncomfortable.

'So, Jamie, what are you working on now?' she asked, and they moved on to talk about architecture and gradually he felt her relax again.

Why? What had Oliver said that had made her tense up like that? Something about her fighting, something significant, something that clearly had affected all of them. Her health issues that she'd been so evasive about? He had no idea what, but he wanted to know.

Later. He'd ask her later.

The party broke up shortly after one when everyone started yawning, and as they paused in the hall to say their goodbyes, she saw Matt and her father deep in conversation and her curiosity was piqued.

'You don't have to thank me, Matt,' her father was saying, his voice soft, but he shook his head.

'I do. Without you...'

Without him, what?

'It was little enough, I was just glad to be

able to help, we both were. I wish we could have done more. And it's great to see you again. Stay in touch this time, eh?'

'I will. And thank you so much for a great party. It's been good to see everyone again. I'm so glad Livvy brought me.'

'So am I, and I'm glad you enjoyed it. Drive carefully, now, she's very precious to us.'

'I'm glad to hear it,' she said, linking her arm through Matt's and wondering what that had all been about. 'Come on, it's time to go. At their age they need their beauty sleep.'

'Cheeky minx,' her father said with a chuckle, and he wrapped her in a firm, warm hug, cradling her against his solid chest as he had done so very many times in her life.

'Love you, Dad,' she said, suddenly welling up, and his arms tightened a fraction before he let her go.

'Love you, too. Take care of her, Matt.'

'I will.'

Their eyes met, her father sending him some warning message, and she tutted at him.

'I can take of myself, Dad. I'm fine.'

She hugged her mother, kissed her brother and sister goodbye and hooked her arm through Matt's.

'Right, let's go.'

* * *

She settled back against the leather, wriggled her feet out of her shoes and glanced across at him. 'Can I ask you something?'

'Only if I can ask you something, too.'

'Me first,' she said, and he gave a resigned laugh.

'Go on, then. Fire away.'

'What did my father do that you thanked him for? It sounded fairly significant.'

'Ah.' He let out a soft huff of breath—almost a laugh, but somehow not, and there was something about it that chilled her. 'It was the day Jules died,' he told her quietly, and her heart sank.

Oh, no...

'We were on a conference in Birmingham and I'd gone up by train, but it was Sunday when it happened and the trains weren't running because of engineering works, so he dropped everything and drove me to London.'

'I didn't realise that. I knew he was with you.'

'Yes. He was amazing. I've never forgotten that, and I've never really thanked him, not properly, so it was good to have the chance because his support made a huge difference.'

She reached out a hand and laid it on his arm, feeling the tension, and guilt racked her.

'I'm so sorry I asked. I can't even imagine what it must have been like for you, but I'm glad he was there and you didn't have to make the journey alone. It must have been awful.'

'It was. And I was very glad he was there, too. So, my turn now.'

'Your turn?'

'To ask you a question.'

'Ah. OK. Fire away,' she said, although she thought she knew what was coming, but fair enough, she'd made him dig out his demons and it was high time she told him.

In the dim light from the instrument panel she saw him glance across at her, then back to the road before he spoke, his voice soft.

'What did your father mean when I said about you having more guts than sense, and he said he knew all about that?'

She gave a forced little laugh, her heart beating faster. 'Nothing. He was just being silly.'

Matt shook his head. 'I don't think so. He didn't sound silly, he sounded deadly serious, as if it was really important. Significant even, to quote you.'

She nodded slowly. He had sounded serious, because he had been, and for good reason. She swallowed, knowing the moment had come, knowing there was nothing she could do but suck it up and tell him.

'Talk to me, Livvy. You said you have health issues. Is that what he was talking about? Are you sick?'

'No. I'm not sick, but I had cancer nearly five years ago.'

'Cancer?'

For a moment he was silent, but then he let his breath out in a long, slow whoosh and pulled over, stopping the car. The interior lights came on automatically, and he twisted round to look at her, his face shocked. 'You had cancer? When you were—what, twenty-four?'

She held his eyes and nodded.

He swore softly, and reached out a hand and cradled her jaw tenderly, his thumb stroking lightly over her cheek in a gentle caress that nearly unravelled her. 'That's tough. That's really tough. How are you now? Are you OK? Are you still having treatment?'

'No—no, I'm fine, they took it out, it's gone and I'm OK. But I've re-evaluated my life and I'm careful with my diet and stuff.'

'Hence the horrible green tea,' he said, and she saw his mouth flicker into a smile that didn't reach his eyes.

She laughed. 'Hence the horrible green tea—although I do actually like it.'

He gave a soft huff of what could have been

laughter, and leant over and feathered a gentle kiss on her lips.

'We're a right pair, aren't we?' he murmured, and then he straightened up and restarted the engine. 'I'd better get you home, Cinderella, before you turn into a pumpkin.'

'I think that was the carriage,' she pointed out drily, and he chuckled, put the car into gear and pulled away.

CHAPTER FIVE

'ARE YOU COMING IN?'

He hesitated, not sure it was a good idea but not sure he could resist.

Not sure he *wanted* to.

'OK, but only for a moment.'

He followed her through the house to the kitchen, and she turned, one hand reaching out to the kettle.

'Coffee?'

'Yeah, please, if you've still got decaf.'

He shrugged off his jacket and hung it over the back of a dining chair, then turned it round and sat and watched her as she spooned the coffee into the cafetière and took out a teabag for herself.

'I might go and change out of this dress while the kettle boils,' she said, heading for the stairs, and he felt an arrow of disappointment.

'That's a pity,' he said, without engaging his brain.

She stopped with her hand on the newel post and looked at him with a puzzled frown. 'Why is it a pity?'

'Because I've been fantasising about taking it off you ever since you opened the door to me,' he said softly, throwing away the last shred of his common sense, and her eyes widened, her lips parted and he watched, mesmerised, as her chest rose and fell a little faster.

So beautiful. So very, very lovely...

Her arm fell back to her side, and she took a step towards him. 'Funny, that,' she said, a tiny smile flickering on soft, moist lips that he was aching to feel with his own. 'I've been thinking the same about your shirt.'

Their eyes locked, and his breath left his body in a rush.

'Livvy?'

He wasn't sure who moved first, but then she was in his arms and he was holding her close and breathing in the scent of her, so warm, so vibrant, so alive.

She'd had cancer. How? Why, when she was so young?

He lifted his head, tilted her face up to his and touched his mouth to hers.

She moaned softly and parted her lips, and he did what he'd been aching to do all evening. He cradled her face in his hands and plundered her mouth, revelling in the taste, the texture, the heat of her breath as she gasped, the press of her body against his, firm and toned and yet still yielding, pliant, all woman.

And he wanted her in a way he'd never thought he'd want again.

He lifted his head and stared down into her eyes, searching them for any sign of doubt, any flicker of hesitation, but there was none.

'I want you,' he said gruffly, and she whimpered and closed her eyes.

'I want you, too—so much, but unless you've got a condom stashed in your wallet…'

Disappointment hit him in the gut, and he tilted his head back with a groan of frustration. 'No. No, I haven't. I didn't think we'd— Not so soon.'

She dropped her arms and eased away. 'Then we can't. I can't risk getting pregnant—I mustn't.' And then she dropped the bombshell. 'I'm on tamoxifen.'

'Tamoxifen?'

It was like a bucket of cold water, and he felt the heat drain away, leaving only shock and the need to hold her. He shut his eyes, letting it sink in, and folded her close again.

'You had breast cancer.'

It wasn't a question. The fact that she was on it was enough. But—breast cancer at twenty-four? That was seriously not good news. And it was an oestrogen-responsive cancer, or she wouldn't be on tamoxifen, not at all, and certainly not after five years. Which had a knock-on effect on all manner of things.

He lifted his head, staring down into her eyes, seeing the shadow of fear there behind her bravado, trying to imagine what she must have gone through. Was still going through, because tamoxifen wasn't a picnic…

'Oh, Olivia… Come here.'

He wrapped her in his arms again, cradling her head against his shoulder, and pressed his lips to her hair. 'Forget the coffee. Let's just go to bed.'

'But we can't—'

'Yes, we can, it's fine.'

'Matt, it's not fine, I can't get pregnant, I really can't—'

'Shh, I know that,' he murmured, soothing the panic he could feel rising in her. 'Trust me, Livvy. I'm not going to do anything. I'm too tired to do you justice, anyway. I only want to hold you.'

'Hold me—?' A tiny sob rose in her throat, and he watched her swallow, fighting it back down. And then she nodded, took a step back, gathered up the hem of that beautiful dress that had tormented him all evening and led him up the stairs, past the bathroom and back towards the front of the house.

She obviously hadn't been expecting him to go in her bedroom because there were clothes all over the place, shoes scattered, the bed rumpled.

He didn't care. He wasn't there to check out her housekeeping skills, and as she stood in the middle of the room, looking racked with doubt, he closed the curtains, turned on the bedside light and walked quietly back to her.

'What's wrong?' he asked softly, taking her hands in his, and she shrugged.

'Nothing. I'm being silly. It's just that I don't know how you'll react when you see me naked…'

'Livvy, I'm a surgeon,' he pointed out gently. 'I've done my share of breast surgery, I know what to expect. I also know it'll take guts to show me, and I know you've got that in spades, but maybe you're just not ready yet to share something so intimate with me, but you don't need to if you don't want to, not tonight, and maybe never. That's fine. I'm not asking you to get naked if you don't want to. You can wear whatever you like. All I want is to hold you. Nothing more. I'm not here to judge you, and nothing's going to change the way I feel about you. You can trust me, and if you're not ready to do that yet, either, if you'd rather I went home, then I'll go. It's up to you.'

He held his breath, waiting, and finally she lifted her head and met his eyes.

Why did everyone think she had guts?

Right then, she felt like the biggest coward in the universe, because she didn't even have the courage to take her clothes off in front of him and it wasn't like he'd be shocked by her scars. They weren't even bad in the great scheme of things. But they were *hers*, and she wanted him to want her and he might not, and that made it different.

Maybe later, further down the line, when she knew him better…?

But if she let him go, if she bottled out now, would he ask again? And how would she feel if he didn't?

Gutted.

She held his eyes, trying to read them, looking for pity, but it wasn't there. Compassion, yes, and understanding, but something else, too, something warm and very masculine that sent a tiny shiver of need through her.

'Don't go.'

His eyes flickered with something unreadable. 'Sure?'

She nodded and sucked in a deep breath.

'Yes. Yes, I'm sure,' she said firmly—more firmly than she felt, but obviously enough to convince him because he smiled then, his mouth tilting slightly, then heeled off his shoes and put them neatly side by side.

His trousers were next, folded carefully over the back of the chair, then he unbuttoned his shirt systematically, button by button, his eyes never leaving hers.

Was he doing it to torture her? Because if so, it was working.

He laid the shirt over the trousers, stripped off his socks and tucked them into his shoes and then, in snug jersey shorts that left much too little to the imagination, he walked slowly towards her, and she felt her mouth dry.

'You look a little over-dressed,' he said softly, and then waited while her heart started to beat faster and her courage wavered.

Now what? Because it was one thing *her* seeing her scar and it reinforcing, every day, the fact that she was alive and well and here to tell the tale. It was quite another to show it to someone else. Even someone who knew what to expect. Especially someone whose reaction mattered so much to her.

But she trusted him, and if she was going to be with him he had to see it, so she might as well get it over with. She screwed up her courage again and held his searching gaze.

'So, I thought you wanted to take my dress off?'

His lips parted, and then he laughed softly and closed his eyes for a moment.

'It'll be a pleasure,' he said, his voice a little rough and gravelly, and took that last step towards her.

'Be careful with it,' she warned, and he laughed again and shook his head slowly.

'I'll be careful,' he promised, and she knew he was talking about more than the dress.

Although the dress did seem to be an issue. He frowned as he studied it. 'You might need to give me a clue. I have no idea how it comes off.'

That made her laugh, too, releasing some of the tension, and she obligingly lifted her left arm and pointed to the concealed zip at the side. 'And there's a tiny hook and eye at the top.'

'I've got it,' he said, and gripping the tab, he slid the zip carefully down, inch by inch, until it reached the bottom, his fingers brushing her skin in passing and making her quiver.

'Over your head, or down past your hips?' he asked, and her heart lurched.

'Hips,' she said, knowing what was coming

next because the dress had inbuilt support so the only underwear she had on was a pair of barely there silky shorts. As he lifted his hands the breath jammed in her throat, trapped there by the pounding of her heart, and then he surprised her.

'Turn around,' he said softly, his hands settling on her shoulders and nudging her gently in the right direction.

She turned, confused, and then felt his fingers take hold of the right shoulder and ease it carefully down her arm. She pulled her arm free, and the dress caught on her hips for a moment, then slithered off and puddled round her ankles, leaving her all but naked.

She had an overwhelming urge to cross her arms across her chest, but she swallowed her fear and kept them still.

Trust him...

'Step out of it.'

If she could make her feet move. She lifted one, then the other, her legs shaking slightly, and he eased the dress away. She heard it rustle as he put it down, and then he was back, his hands curving over her shoulders, his fingertips resting on her collarbones, his thumbs sweeping lightly over the back of her neck.

She felt his breath against her nape, then the touch of his mouth, warm and reassuring.

'So let's see how this clip works,' he said, and then his hands were in her hair, freeing it so it tumbled down around her shoulders, and she heard him sigh softly.

'That's better. I love your hair,' he murmured, sifting it through his fingers, and then gently, without exerting any pressure, he turned her back towards him.

'Come here,' he said softly, and drew her into his arms, folding her gently against that broad, reassuringly solid chest. She felt the brush of the soft, dark hair that sprinkled his pecs, the warmth of his skin on hers, smelt the scent of his body overlaid with cologne, warm and slightly musky and enticing.

'That's better,' he murmured, and for a long time he did nothing except hold her. Her heart was pounding—or was it his? His, maybe, strong and steady, and she felt hers settle, but then he lowered his head and trailed a line of kisses over her cheek and down across her shoulder, lifting her hair out of the way, tunnelling his fingers through it and kissing the side of her neck behind her ear, sending flames licking through her.

Then he let her go, slid his hands down her arms and linked his fingers with hers as he took a step back and looked slowly down, and she closed her eyes and waited, her heart racing now.

'Look at me,' he murmured, and she opened her eyes and stared straight into his. They were dark, darker than she'd ever seen them, the colour of wet slate, his pupils flared, and his chest was rising and falling with every breath.

'You're beautiful, Olivia,' he said, his voice raw, 'absolutely beautiful,' and her heart turned over. Nobody had ever said that to her before—well, only her parents and that didn't count, not in this way. Not in the way he'd said it, and she felt her eyes fill.

'Come here,' he murmured, and she took a deep breath and stepped into his arms.

'That feels so good.'

His voice was a low murmur, his breath drifting against her skin as they lay tangled together in her bed. He scattered tiny, nibbling kisses over her face, and Livvy closed her eyes. She could feel the need in him, in the rise and fall of his chest, the pounding of his heart, the hard jut of his erection against her body. She moaned and moved closer, their legs meshing, but that just made the ache worse. 'I want you.'

'I want you, too, but we can't.'

'I know. I'm so cross. Why didn't we think ahead?'

He laughed unsteadily, his hand cradling her face, his thumb stroking her cheek rhythmically, soothing her. 'Because we didn't have an agenda,' he said. 'And because I guess we're both out of practice and it didn't even occur to us that this might happen so soon, even though we'd had that conversation. I'm sorry. I just didn't expect it, and I didn't realise—I just thought you might be on the pill or something.'

She nodded. It certainly hadn't occurred to her, and she was kicking herself for that because she'd expected him to have thought of it.

'I can't take the pill, and even if I could, I wouldn't need to be on it. There hasn't been anyone, not since...'

'Not at all?'

She shook her head. 'No. The guy I was with then really couldn't handle it, our relationship wasn't strong enough, so I ended it, and since then I haven't been ready—physically, emotionally. But I'm ready now, and we can't, and that's my fault.' She laid a hand against his cheek, feeling the tingle of stubble, the hard line of his jaw, the clench of a muscle. 'I'm sorry.'

'You have nothing to be sorry for,' he said gently, sifting his fingers through her hair now, his eyes on hers. 'Nothing. And there's no hurry.'

His mouth found hers again, and she felt heat race through her like a wildfire, reaching every part of her and making her whimper. She reached for him, her hand sliding down his chest, but he caught her wrist and stopped her.

'Uh-uh,' he murmured. 'You can't do that, Livvy. I'm hanging by a thread as it is and when we do this, I want to do it properly, not when we're both tired and we can't follow through.'

His fingers traced her cheek, and his smile was gentle and a bit wry. 'I think it's time we went to sleep, don't you?'

He reached out and turned off the light, then gathered her up against his chest and kissed her again, a tender, gentle kiss, cooling the heat but filling her with a different sort of warmth that brought tears to her eyes.

She settled against him, her head on his shoulder, and as she lay there she could hear his heartbeat slow, taking hers with it as she drifted peacefully into sleep.

He woke shortly before seven and got up, pulled on his clothes and brought her a cup of green tea, kissing her awake.

She blinked and stared at him. 'You're dressed! What time is it?'

'Seven. I need to go. I'm going to be conspicuous enough going home in these clothes, but the later I leave it the worse it'll be because there'll be more people about.'

'You'll just meet all the runners and dog walkers getting out before it's too hot,' she told him, and he had a horrible feeling she was right, but it had to be done and, anyway, the children would ring him soon and he needed to be able to talk to them without distractions or they'd be curious. Or Sally would, and he wasn't ready to tell Sally about this—whatever this was—when he was still coming to terms with it himself.

Besides, he needed to go shopping.

'Look, I have to go. Why don't you get up when you're ready and have a shower and then come round to mine? I'll feed you brunch.'

'Scrambled egg club sandwich?'

He chuckled and kissed her again. 'Of course. Bring some green tea, I don't have any and they might not have any in the little shop. Do you know where I live?'

She shook her head.

'I'll text you my address when I get home. It's on the clifftop near Ed and Annie, on the way to the harbour. Ring me when you leave.'

'OK. I'll see you later—about nine?'

'Sounds fine.'

And it would have been, if he hadn't bumped

into Ed. He'd been walking their dog along the clifftop, and he crossed the road and paused on the drive as Matt got out of the car.

'Morning! Another gorgeous day.'

He stifled a groan and patted the dog, who was nudging his hand. 'Isn't it a bit early to be so cheerful?'

'This is early?' Ed said with a laugh. 'The kids have been up an hour, and I always walk the dog first thing, you know that.' He eyed his clothes pointedly. 'Good party?' he added with all the subtlety of an express train, and Matt sighed.

'Yes, thanks. Bit of a late night, though.'

'So how *is* Livvy? I take it she's got over her fall?' he asked.

How the hell—? Unless it was just a random punt...

'She's fine. She's coming over shortly for brunch so I can't hang about, I need to go shopping.'

'She's nice. I like her,' Ed said casually, but there was nothing casual about it and he had to stop himself from rolling his eyes. 'She's also very kind and soft-hearted,' he added quietly. 'Don't hurt her, Matt.'

He stopped trying to get away and turned to face his old friend. 'Why would you think I'd hurt her?'

Ed shook his head, his eyes serious now. 'I don't know, but your car was outside her house fifteen minutes ago and you're not exactly dressed for a lazy Sunday morning, so I'm guessing you spent the night with her.'

He held on to his temper with difficulty. 'How is that in any way your business?'

'It isn't. I know that, but I care about you, Matt, and I care about Livvy, and I'd hate to see either of you get hurt. Just be sure you're ready for this before you get in too deep—unless it's just casual sex, but I really hope not. You've had a tough time, and I'm glad you're moving on, but I'd hate to think you were using her to do it.'

'I'm not *using* her,' he said firmly, slamming the car door and walking off before he said something he'd regret, but his friend's words had struck a chord, and he went into the house and closed the door with a shaky sigh.

Was Ed right? Was he using her? No. Surely not. That wasn't how it felt at all, but how did it feel?

Crazy, immense, confusing.

And hugely important, somehow. So the other thing, then. Was Ed right about that, about him getting in too deep, too soon? And too deep for who? Him, still mourning the loss of Jules, or Olivia, still dealing with the after-math of cancer?

Both of them, probably, but Ed's less than subtle warning had come too late, because he was in it up to his neck now and there was no way he could walk away from her even if he wanted to. And he didn't want to.

What about the children?

What about them? They weren't part of this—this whatever it was. Arrangement? It wasn't even that organised.

He went into his bedroom, sent her a text message with his address, then showered slowly, pulled on shorts and a T-shirt, tidied the house a bit and headed out to the near-est express store. It had just opened, and he grabbed food for breakfast and a few other essentials.

Something for him and the kids tonight, salad, more ketchup—and condoms? He hesi-tated, staring blankly at the display, wondering at the wisdom of it. If he bought them, they'd use them. If he didn't, they'd wait.

Maybe that was a good idea, just until he'd worked out what the hell he was doing and why.

He left them on the shelf and headed for the checkout.

* * *

Her phone was ringing as she got out of the shower, and she grabbed her towel, scrubbed her hands dry and picked it up, putting it on hands-free so she could dry herself while she talked.

'Hi, Dad, you're up bright and early. How are you? How's the head?'

He laughed, the sound echoing round the bathroom. 'My head's fine, thank you. How's yours?'

'Oh, fine. I'm tired, but I'm OK. It was a great party.'

'It was, wasn't it? Your mother's good at that sort of thing. So, I take it you got home all right?'

Her heart gave a little lurch.

'Yes, fine, thanks. We got back about two. Matt was very pleased to have seen you both and had a chance to thank you for what you did for him. I knew you'd been there, but I didn't realise you'd driven him to London that day. It must have been awful.'

'He told you about it?'

'Only that, really. Not much at all.'

'No, I don't suppose he did. He probably finds it hard to talk about. Livvy, darling, you will be careful, won't you? Don't let yourself get too involved. He won't mean to hurt you, he's not like that, but he was devastated when his wife died and he can't be in a good place even now, and there are the children to consider as well, and I know that's an issue for you. Just be careful and don't let yourself get in too deep.'

Too late...

'Dad, I'm fine. Don't worry about me, or him, or the children. Neither of us is looking for anything serious and I know it's not going anywhere. Look, I don't mean to be rude but we've arranged to meet up for breakfast and I'm just out of the shower and I need to dry my hair.'

'OK, but take care. I love you.'

'Love you, too.'

She rang Matt as she left home, and he was just getting the shopping out of his car when she pulled up on the drive outside his house. His very impressive, beautifully presented clifftop house that made her little rented Victorian semi seem very tame.

'Hi,' she said, going over to him, and he bent and kissed her cheek.

'Hi. You OK?'

'Yes, I'm fine, thanks. A bit tired still, but that goes with the territory, I'm often tired. So, what's in the shopping bag?'

'Bacon, eggs, tomatoes, bread and some other bits and pieces. I really need to do a proper internet order if I ever get a minute, but I did manage to get green tea for you so I'm not entirely useless. Come on in.'

She wondered what else he'd bought and if he'd remedied their tragic failure to think ahead. Maybe. She could only hope.

She followed him through the door and into a huge L-shaped living space that ran across the house and from front to back, with stunning views down the drive and across the cliff-top to the sea, and her eyes widened. 'Oh, wow. That's amazing. I can see why you bought it.'

He gave a hollow laugh and dumped the shopping on the worktop.

'To be honest, eighteen months ago the sea view was the last thing on my mind, but it ticked all the boxes. It's got four bedrooms, it's literally just round the corner from my mother, who is utterly indispensable to me and the children, and it has the added bonus of a garage I can convert into an annex for her if and when necessary, so it was exactly what I needed, but it was in a shocking state and I poured a lot of money and effort into it without really thinking about anything but the practicalities.'

He smiled wryly. 'And then suddenly I had time to stop and look out of the window and, yes, it's amazing. There's a balcony outside my bedroom and I sit there often, just staring out over the sea, listening to the gulls and the waves breaking on the shore and watching the world go by.'

'I could do a lot of that,' she said wistfully. 'I love the sound of the sea. I'm not sure I'd swap it for my oasis, though.'

'I wouldn't, I love your garden. Mine'll get there one day, I suppose, when everything's grown a bit, but in the meantime I do have a great view so I'm not exactly deprived. And of course ultimately I'll end up with both. So— scrambled, I take it?'

'Of course.' She dragged her eyes off the view and turned to face him with a smile. 'Anything I can do to help?'

He opened the folding doors across the front of the kitchen and they ate their club sandwiches perched at the breakfast bar.

She licked her fingers, pushed the plate away and sighed contentedly. 'That was amazing. I haven't had a club sandwich that good for ages.'

'Is that because it's on your anti-cancer hit list?' he asked, and she laughed and shook her head.

'No, not really. It's not great, and I wouldn't

do it every day, but in the grand scheme of things it's not bad. Top of my hit list is sugar because cancer loves it apparently, followed by anything fed with hormones or too much Omega 6, plus high glycaemic index foods like white rice and flour and stuff like that, so no dairy, no cakes, no puddings, nothing with added sugar, although I do eat a lot of fruit. Oh, and loads of fresh veg and extra virgin olive oil and lots and lots of fish, and organic produce as a rule when I can, and I don't drink alcohol any more. And I make sure I exercise and get lots of fresh air.'

'Sounds pretty healthy.'

'It is. I do draw the line at revolting super-green smoothies, though,' she added with a wry grin, and he chuckled.

'I can't *imagine* why. Ugh.'

'Ugh is an understatement. Have you ever had one? They taste like grass mowings.' She put her mug down and swivelled round to face him. 'Can I be cheeky and ask for a guided tour?'

He shrugged and slid off his stool.

'Sure. It's not that exciting.'

Well, it might not be to him, but a sea view like that was her idea of heaven and she was aching to see what he'd done with the rest of the house.

He walked her through the downstairs first—a utility room, cloakroom, another sitting room that opened to the garden, with lots of toy storage and comfy sofas, the walls smothered in children's paintings lovingly pinned up, all named and dated, and then on the opposite wall were framed black-and-white photos of the children, which gave her a pang of longing that she quickly suppressed.

The children weren't part of this, they weren't relevant, only insofar as they governed what time she and Matt could spend together, so she hauled her eyes off them and followed him out of the room.

He took her upstairs next and then, as if to turn the screw, he showed her the children's rooms—a delicate blue, surprisingly, for Amber, and white with a mural of trains stuck on it for Charlie—then the guest room, which his mother used when he was on call, he said, and the family bathroom, obviously tastefully refitted, although the effect was trashed by the addition of about a million bath toys.

She could hear the squeals of laughter, the splashing, the giggles, and the ache in her chest just grew worse.

They're nothing to do with you.

Then finally he led her into his bedroom,

and she heaved a silent sigh of relief because this was undoubtedly an adult room.

It was the largest, as she might have expected, with a huge and incredibly inviting bed opposite a wall of glass giving a stunning view of the sea and sky, and it took her breath away.

What would it be like to lie there with him, to make love in that huge bed with the sound of the sea drifting in through the open doors? To sit on the balcony and listen to the keening of the gulls, and then go back to bed and make love again...

'That's amazing,' she breathed. 'What an incredible room. You must get fabulous sunrises.'

'I do, but I see them rather too often at the moment, considering it rises at four thirty at this time of year,' he said drily.

'That's horribly early! Why are you awake then?'

He gave a wry chuckle.

'I'm not. It's Charlie. Sometimes he wakes up needing to wee and won't settle again unless he's with me, but just lately I've been getting the bed to myself most nights, which is a real luxury. I still wake up, though. Habit.'

She laughed, as she was meant to, but her mind was torn between the yearning to hold a little wakeful boy and cradle him back to sleep, and wondering what it would be like to wake up to the sunrise with Matt and make love with the first rays of light gilding their bodies...

And then she glanced across the room at the chest of drawers on the far side, and stopped.

Stopped thinking about the children, stopped fantasising about spending one of those uninterrupted nights with him in that huge and inviting bed, stopped wondering if he'd bought condoms, stopped thinking about his body underneath those shorts.

Stopped thinking altogether, because there on the chest of drawers in a simple white frame was a black-and-white photo of a woman holding a sleeping baby in her arms, and tucked in beside her was a little girl with Matt's eyes and her long dark hair. Amber, of course. She recognised her from the photos downstairs, but the woman... They were both smiling, and Livvy felt as if a giant hand had squeezed her heart.

'That's Juliet with the children,' he said softly, his voice tender. 'It was taken just after Christmas, five months before she died.'

She swallowed and turned away, unable to look at it any longer because it felt such an intrusion into his privacy and grief. Before it had just been a bedroom, and Juliet hadn't had a face, and now it all seemed much more real, the scale of his loss, the agonising grief he must have gone through, still be going through. The children's grief and loss, the loss of their mother, irreplaceable and so much loved.

She didn't belong there...

'I'm sorry—'

'Don't be. She's gone, Olivia. I know that. I still love her, I always will, but she's gone, and I'm getting used to it. It's just taking me a while.'

She nodded, swallowing again, blinking away the sudden, stinging tears. 'Dad phoned this morning and warned me not to get in too deep, said you couldn't be in a good place right now. He was right, wasn't he?'

He gave a soft huff of laughter and turned away from the picture, ushering her out of the door and down the stairs.

'That depends what you call good. I've sold our house in London, found a new home, a new job, a new life. I'm moving on, slowly but surely, so I'm in a better place than I was, that's for sure. I wouldn't want to go back to those early days.'

She shook her head. 'I'm so sorry, Matt. It must have been awful.'

'It was, but I'm getting there. Come and see the garden.'

He opened a door at the end of the hall and went out, and she followed him slowly, wondering what she was doing there and how she'd got into this. And—the garden? That was such an abrupt change of subject...

She stopped. 'Do you want me to go?'

'Go? No, of course not. Why would I want you to go?' he asked, but then he turned and looked at her, and with a sigh he pulled her into his arms and hugged her, and she wrapped her arms around him and hung on.

CHAPTER SIX

FOR A WHILE he said nothing, then he gave a sigh and lifted his head and looked down at her, his eyes troubled.

'It's not just your father who's worried about us. I got lectured today as well,' he said. 'I met Ed on my way home this morning while he was walking the dog. He'd been past your house earlier, seen the car there and knew I hadn't been home, and of course I was in those clothes, so he said he was glad to see I was moving on but then told me rather pointedly that you have a kind heart and I'm not to hurt you by getting in too deep before I'm ready.'

'You won't hurt me,' she said, not altogether sure it was true. Well, she was sure *he* wouldn't hurt her. Whether the situation would hurt her was another question entirely, and one she'd rather not consider because she didn't think she'd like the answer. Although if her reaction to the children's pictures was anything to go by, she had her answer already.

'I hope not. Ed also said he hoped I wasn't using you and I told him I'm not. If I am it's entirely unintentional, anyway, and if you feel I am, then for goodness' sake tell me, because it's the last thing on earth I want to do.'

She lifted her hand and cradled his jaw, feeling the prickle of stubble against her palm, the flicker of a muscle in his cheek. 'You're not using me, Matt. Not in the least.'

He turned his head and pressed his lips to her palm, then gave a wry little laugh and moved, putting a little space between them, although he held on to her hand, folding it inside his.

'Good. I really don't want to, which is why I didn't buy condoms this morning. I didn't want to railroad either you or myself into something rash, and now I'm regretting it.'

She shook her head and gave him a wistful smile. 'Don't regret it. Just be sure you're ready, Matt. There's no hurry and I don't want you doing something you're not ready for, something that will make you feel disloyal to Juliet or that you're cheating her or that I don't measure up.'

He frowned. 'I wouldn't feel that, Olivia, and I wouldn't for a moment compare you to her. We had a good marriage, a brilliant marriage, and I wouldn't for the world have had it end the way it did, but it has, and she's gone, but I'm still here and so are the children, and we're all entitled to a life, even if it's a very different one from the one we'd thought we'd have. She'd be furious with me if I passed up any chance for happiness, however fleeting, and she'd be the last one to want me to be lonely. She would have hated that for me.'

Livvy felt her eyes fill. 'She sounds lovely. You must miss her so much.'

He smiled sadly. 'I do. I miss her every day, but life goes on, and I'm still alive, and since I met you I feel I've come out of the shadows and into the light again, and d'you know what? It feels good, Livvy. It feels really good, and that's all down to you.'

He led her to a faded, weathered bench tucked in a corner between the house and the newly planted shrubs, and patted the seat beside him.

'Come and sit with me. This is a lovely bench, the only thing I have from our London garden, and I don't spend anything like enough time on it any more, but all I can see from it now is emptiness and a lawn that needs cutting, so I look at the trees next door instead.' He grinned wryly. 'You have to tilt your head back a bit, so you can end up with a crick in your neck if you're not careful.'

She smiled and sat down beside him—had Juliet sat on this bench with him? Probably—and she looked at the trees for a moment, then her smile faded and she turned to face him, her mind still on Juliet and his tragic loss.

'I don't want to take you back into the shadows, but can I ask you something?'

He turned his head and met her eyes. 'Of course you can. You can ask me anything.'

'What happened that day? How did you know she was ill?'

He sighed and looked away again, back to the trees that seemed to give him comfort. 'I didn't,' he said quietly. 'I'd spoken to her the night before and she had a headache. The children had been noisy all day, she said, and her head was banging and as they were asleep she was going to get an early night. It didn't sound like anything out of the ordinary, because she'd had the odd headache from time to time, as we all do, so I said good idea, went in to dinner, and I rang her in the morning for our usual catch-up and I couldn't get hold of her.

'It didn't really worry me, I assumed she was busy with the children and she'd ring me when she could, and I had a breakfast meeting scheduled with your father and a few others so I showered and dressed and went down to the dining room, and then I still hadn't heard from her, so I rang again, then I rang her mobile, then the house phone again, and Amber answered.'

'Amber?' she asked, shocked. 'How old was she?'

He shrugged. 'Two and three quarters? Something like that. I could hear Charlie screaming in the background and I thought Jules must be dealing with a stinky nappy or something, so I asked to speak to her and Amber told me Mummy wouldn't get up and she was talking funny.'

'Oh, Matt,' she murmured, feeling sick at the thought. 'So what did you do?'

He shrugged again. 'What could I do? I was a hundred miles away and I didn't know what the hell was going on, I just knew it wasn't good. I couldn't even ring the neighbours, I didn't know their numbers, Jules had all that sort of stuff, so I asked Amber where her mother was and she said she was in bed, and Charlie wanted his bottle and she was hungry, too, so I asked her to take the phone to her mother and hold it by her ear, and Jules made this odd mumbling sort of noise and I knew then that it was really bad. I told her not to worry, that I'd get help and just hang in there, I'd be home as soon as I could.

'Your father was with me by then, and he just took over. He'd heard what I'd said, seen my face, could hear Charlie screaming, and he dialled 999, told them the situation, handed me his phone and told me to direct them to the house, then took my phone off me and talked calmly to Amber while we headed back to our rooms. He packed his things and mine, still talking to Amber while I was on the phone to the police, and then he put me in his car and started driving.'

'So where was your car?'

'At home, because I'd gone by train, but I would have been in no fit state to drive anyway, so he handed me back my phone and drove like the wind while I talked to Amber again, and to the police on his hands-free until they got into the house, then they told me the paramedics were in and they were taking her to hospital, and Amber said a nice lady was there and she was going to get them breakfast, so I told her to be brave and look after Charlie and help the lady to find all their things and I'd see her soon, and then I rang Juliet's mother and told her to get to the hospital, put the phone down and fell apart, and he just kept driving and talking to me, calming me down, keeping me sane.

'He called your mother and got her to come down on the train from Suffolk, and they looked after the children with the police while I went in to see Jules in ICU. She was in a coma, one pupil fixed and dilated, and as I watched the other one blew and I knew she was gone. I never got to say goodbye, and that still hurts. If I'd known when I spoke to her that it would be the last time—'

His voice cracked a little, and she reached out a hand and squeezed his wordlessly, because there were no words she could have used. He blinked and looked up, staring up at the trees and probably seeing something else entirely. Then he hauled in a breath and started again.

'They did brain-stem tests but they were all dire, and in the end your father was the one who broached the subject of organ donation. He knew Jules and I were both doctors, and he knew her, knew what she was like, knew she wouldn't have wanted her body to go to waste, and he was right to raise it with me, because she would have come back to haunt me if I hadn't done it.'

He swallowed. 'I baulked at it at first, and then I thought of the people out there desperate for a transplant, and that maybe it would give them a chance to live a normal life, so I said yes, use everything they could, and I know her heart and lungs went to a teenager with cystic fibrosis, and her kidneys went to two people in their thirties with end-stage renal failure. I don't know about all the other organs, but I just know that in a way Jules is still out there somewhere, giving other people a chance at what she'd lost. That's a huge comfort.'

Livvy felt a tear slide down her cheek and swiped it away. How could he be so strong, so brave? She'd be in bits. He said he had been. Maybe he still was, and maybe her father and Ed were right?

'Anyway,' he added after a long pause, 'your parents were wonderful, and without their kindness and support I don't know how I would have got through that day. They stayed with the children until my mother came, and then I had to tell Amber her mother was never coming home. That was the hardest thing I've ever done in my life—'

He broke off again, and she squeezed his hand, unable to speak.

'So, anyway, that's why I wanted to thank them. For that, and for all the kindness they'd showed us over the years, the welcome they gave Juliet when I was his registrar—all of it.

I can't even begin to explain how much it all meant, how much it still means, and I've never really told them.'

She didn't know what to say, so she said nothing, just leant over and hugged him, her eyes squeezed tightly shut, and he wrapped her in his arms and held her for an age. And then finally he lifted his head and sighed.

'Sorry. That was a bit heavy. I didn't mean to spill my guts like that but you did ask.'

She nodded, blinking hard. 'I know. I'm sorry. I should have realised it wasn't a simple question. I didn't mean to make you dredge all that back up, I'm really sorry.'

She felt his shoulders shift in a little shrug. 'It's OK. It's never very far away. So, your turn now, talking of dredging things up. How did you find out you had cancer?'

She sat up, swiped the tears away and laughed at that, because it seemed somehow trivial and insignificant in comparison to what he'd gone through, although at the time it had seemed horrendous and insurmountable and maybe still did, when she let herself think about it, which was why she didn't, because otherwise she'd crumble.

And she wasn't going to let herself do that.

'I felt it,' she told him, trying to sound matter-of-fact, 'this tiny little bump. It was so small, like a little pea, but just enough to feel. I was very thin at the time, I'd been living on fresh air and nerves through my finals, and I was just getting to the end of my F1 year, my first year in the real world, and I was in the shower and I felt this little thing up near my armpit, so I went to see my GP thinking it was just a gland, I was run-down, it was nothing, and he said it needed investigating and referred me urgently, which freaked me out a bit, so as soon as I got my mammogram appointment I contacted the breast clinic and pointed out I worked in the hospital so I was available at no notice if they had a cancellation, and two days later they rang me to say someone had broken down on the way and could I take the appointment, and three days after that they called me back in, did a million more tests and told me I had cancer.'

He swore softly and threaded his fingers through hers. 'And then what?'

She laughed. 'They did a lumpectomy, but the pathologist said they hadn't taken enough margin so six weeks later after it was healed I had to have another op, and then when it was healed again I had radiotherapy. They'd taken four lymph nodes, and they were all clear, so I didn't need chemo. I was very relieved about that because I was dreading it, but anyway, it healed, I was fine, and I got on with it, but it was pretty grim and I took a year out just to come to terms with it because it shakes you, you know? You feel nothing's the same any more, and you suddenly realise who your friends are and who matters and who doesn't, and what things are important and what's just white noise, and you cut all that out of your life. Like Mark.'

'Mark?'

'My ex. He didn't want to know, and if he didn't want to know, I didn't want him there, so I cut him out of my life. I read a ton of books about self-help, diet, fitness—'

'Hence the green tea and the sugar ban,' he said softly, and she smiled and nodded.

'Hence the green tea and the sugar ban and all the other stuff. And you know, I feel better than I ever have? I'm fit, I'm well, my work-life balance is better, I sleep well now, I don't do things that make me stressed or unhappy, and every day I get up and count my blessings—number one being that I'm still here.'

Even if I'm alone because I can't drag anyone with me on this crazy roller coaster, and even if I'll never be able to have a child...

He gave a soft huff of laughter. 'Yeah, I absolutely get that. Life's pretty fragile. You've only got to do our job to realise that, but you can get immune to it and then it comes home to roost and it's quite a wake-up call. It's certainly given me a better insight into how to give bad news because I know now what it feels like to be on the receiving end of it, and it ain't pretty.'

He sighed, and glanced at his watch.

'I need to go soon, I'm having lunch with the children at Juliet's sister's, but we've got time for another drink if you'd like?'

'Are you sure?' She turned to face him, searching his eyes, but they were puzzled.

'Why wouldn't I be sure?'

She shrugged. 'I don't know. Because talking about her upset you, and that's my fault and I thought you might want me to go.'

'No. I wanted you to know, and I wanted to know about you, and I certainly don't want you to go. It's all good.' He slung an arm around her shoulders, dropped a quick kiss on her lips and pulled her to her feet.

'Come on, let's go and get another drink and soak up some of that gorgeous sea view you're raving about, and then we can talk about when we're going to squeeze in another date—assuming you still want to, now you know what a sad case I am?'

She stared at him as if he was crazy. 'Of course I want to! Well, if you do...'

'Oh, I do,' he said, his eyes curiously intent. 'I definitely do.' His mouth quirked. 'But I might need to go shopping.'

She felt the tension shift and the atmosphere lighten, and she smiled back at him.

'I'm so glad you said that.'

He laughed, swore softly under his breath and kissed her, then let her go and stepped away. 'Don't look at me like that! It's difficult enough. Right, let's get this drink before we do something stupid.'

It was so simple in theory, but in practice finding time to get together when both of them were free and his mother could babysit was next to impossible, and it was frustrating him to bits.

He worked mostly days except for when he was on call or on the weekend rota, and Livvy was on a phase of late shifts, so it was Friday before they caught up face-to-face.

He was called down to the ED to look at a young man who'd been slashed by a bottle in a drunken brawl at five in the afternoon, and he found her in a cubicle, applying pressure to the wound while the man gripped her by the wrist and yelled abuse.

'Problems?' he asked her, but the patient answered.

'Stupid woman's hurting me, I want a doctor, not a reg—whatever it says on her badge!' he yelled, and Matt calmly prised his fingers off her wrist, placed a hand on his chest and pinned him firmly to the bed.

'Then you'd better behave. Either you need our help,' he went on, his voice deadly quiet, 'or you leave, but we don't take that sort of abuse from anybody, under any circumstances, and you either apologise to *Dr* Henderson now or I call Security and you leave and take your chances, but you've already lost a lot of blood so I don't fancy the odds. The choice is yours.'

'But she doesn't know what she's doing!'

'Dr Henderson knows *exactly* what she's doing, and right now she's trying to stop you bleeding to death, so the least you can do is be a little co-operative while she does it,' he said tightly. He felt the man slump under his hand, and he nodded. 'Right, let's start again. My name's Matthew Hunter—'

He tensed again. 'It says you're Mister on your badge! That's not a proper doctor, either!'

'Mr Hunter is a consultant trauma surgeon,' Livvy said crisply, 'and I only called him down because he's a soft-tissue injury specialist, so you should consider yourself very, very lucky to have him and start to co-operate before he refuses to treat you.'

He opened his mouth, shut it and let out a huff.

'Better,' Matt said, stifling a smile at Livvy's skilful and cutting intervention. 'Now apologise to her,' he added, and the man grumbled what might just have been an apology, and he let him go.

'Right, if we're all done with the drama let's have a look at this,' he said, snapping on gloves, and Livvy moved out of the way and he lifted the saturated pad and slapped it back on.

'OK, he's nicked an artery, we need to move to Resus.'

'An artery? Isn't that dangerous?' the man said, his eyes widening.

'Only if we let go. You need to pick your fights more carefully.'

'It wasn't me who did it, it was my mate,' the man said, looking worried now and missing his double meaning, and Matt stifled a laugh.

'You need to pick your friends more carefully, then. Right, let's move,' he said, and holding pressure on the leg, he kicked the brakes off and helped shift him through to Resus.

It took nearly an hour for him to repair the leg to his satisfaction, but finally the man was shipped out to the observation cubicles and he had a minute to talk to Livvy alone.

He ushered her out of Resus and into the corridor.

'How can they get in that much trouble in the middle of the afternoon?' he grumbled, and she laughed.

'Tell me about it. Anyway, enough of him. How are you?' she asked, looking up at him with a smile, and his mouth tilted.

'Much better now he's gone and I've got you to myself. What are you doing tomorrow evening?'

'Tomorrow? Nothing.'

'So do you fancy going out for a meal?'

Her eyes lit up. 'That would be lovely. Or I could cook for you?'

He shook his head. 'No. That would make me a liar. I told my mother there was a possibility a couple of people from the hospital were going to the pub,' he said with a wry grin, and her mouth formed a little O, and then she smiled.

'In which case, the pub would be great. Do you want me to meet you there?'

'No. I'll pick you up but I haven't decided where we're going yet. Seafront, river or country?' he asked.

'Ooh, that's tough. River?'

He nodded. 'I know the perfect place. Eight o'clock OK?'

She smiled up into his eyes, and his heart started to beat a little faster.

'Sounds perfect. Is it dressy?'

He shook his head. 'No. We did that last week. This is definitely casual. I'll probably wear jeans and a shirt. Right, I need to get home. I'm already late. See you tomorrow.'

He glanced around to make sure there was nobody watching, then dropped a kiss on her lips, winked and walked away, his heart lighter and his body humming with anticipation.

The house was quiet when he got home, and he found his mother in the family room, picking up toys.

'Here, let me.' He got down on his knees to help her. 'I'm sorry I'm late. How've they been?'

'Oh, fine. I told them you'd go up and see them when you got back, and they were quite happy.' She stacked the last of the toys on the shelves and straightened up. 'So, is this pub thing on tomorrow night, or don't you know yet?'

He got to his feet and busied himself straightening the pile of books on the shelf. Not that they needed it.

'Yes, it is, if that's all right? I was about to ask you. I need to leave just before eight, but

I'll make sure they're in bed by then, and I won't be late.'

What was it about mothers? She added another book to his pile, tilted her head on one side, frowned and said, 'Matthew, look at me,' in that voice she'd used since he was about three and she'd caught him raiding the chocolate biscuits.

He gave an inward sigh and met her eyes, wondering what she'd see. Too much, probably.

Definitely. 'You are allowed a life, darling,' she said softly after a long, long moment. 'I really don't mind babysitting so you can go and have fun. And if you like, I'll have them for a sleepover. They haven't been for a few weeks, and Amber was asking about it yesterday. Then you wouldn't need to worry about getting back early, or even at all,' she added, her voice laden with meaning.

He felt his eyes fill for no very good reason, and looked away again. 'Are you sure?'

'Yes, I'm sure. I take it this is Oliver Henderson's daughter?'

How had she known that? Except of course she knew they'd been on the team-building thing together, and he'd taken her to the party. Not to mention babysitting so he could have that sneaky little coffee in her garden—their first date, if you could call it that. Blindingly obvious, really, and he should have realised she'd guess. Unless Ed had been shooting his mouth off...

He nodded. 'Yes. Yes, it is.' He sighed and dragged a hand through his hair and turned back to face her again, the whole situation suddenly overwhelming him. 'I don't know where it's going, and I know it's too soon, but—Mum, she's had breast cancer—'

'Breast cancer?' she echoed, shocked, and he nodded.

'Yes, I know, and she's only twenty-nine now, and she's so matter-of-fact, and so positive and proactive and just—just *so* brave. It's heartbreaking listening to her, because she brushes it aside and says it's fine, but you know it's not fine, she was so young, and—'

He broke off, and his mother took his arm gently. 'Oh, darling. Are you sure it's wise getting involved with her?'

He gave a huff of laughter without a shred of humour because it was so unfunny.

'What, because she might die, too? It's highly unlikely, she says they got it all and she should know, but in any case I can't live my life thinking like that even if it wasn't all right. We all have to die at some point, but that doesn't mean we don't deserve to be happy in the meantime. And there's something about her that makes me happy, and I haven't been happy for two years, Mum. And I want to be, even if it's foolish, even if I'm setting myself up for heartbreak all over again, because I just want to be with her. I need to be with her, and I think she needs to be with me, at least for now, and if I can make her happy, too, then that's all I can ask.'

She studied him thoughtfully. 'That sounds as if you're thinking long-term.'

'It does, doesn't it?' he murmured, examining that thought. 'I don't know. Maybe I am. I just know I want to be with her. I haven't got any further than that yet, but I wouldn't be surprised.'

'And where do the children fit into all this?'

He stared at her, a hollow feeling in his chest. 'I don't know. It's a good question and one I keep asking myself, but I can't answer it right now because I honestly don't have a clue, because I really wasn't expecting to feel like this so I'm totally unprepared for it and I don't know what to do. I have to protect the children, I know that, but what about her? Doesn't she deserve to be happy? Don't I? And I don't know where it's going, I just know she means a lot to me and I can't walk away.'

'Oh, Matthew...'

Her arms went round him, and he hugged

her close, his eyes tightly shut, because she of all people knew what might lie ahead. She'd nursed his father till he'd died of cancer, supported him through the chemo, the tests, the new chemo, another one, the palliative operations, the endless cycle of hope and despair, and then she'd buried him, heartbroken and yet relieved that finally his pain was over.

So she knew exactly what might lie ahead for him if it all went wrong, and for the children, and he felt her body shudder as he held her. And then she pushed him away, cupped his head in her hands and kissed his cheek, her eyes brimming with tears.

'You're a brave man, Matthew. You remind me so much of your father. That's exactly what he'd say.'

Then she let him go, sniffed hard and straightened her shoulders and headed for the kitchen. 'I've made a chicken and bacon salad for you. It's in the fridge, and there's some olive ciabatta to go with it, and we went to the farm shop and picked some raspberries. They're in the fridge, too. So, shall I pick the children up at five thirty tomorrow in time for supper?'

Livvy spent the rest of her hectic Friday night shift dealing with abusive drunks and silly kids who'd overindulged, and then a girl of fifteen was brought in in a state of collapse after taking something at a party, and Livvy was the first to see her.

She immediately called James Slater, their clinical lead, and she was relieved when she heard the door swish open behind her.

'OK, what have we got?' he asked.

'This is Kelly, she's fifteen, she's got rigid muscles, shallow breathing, heart rate's one-sixty, she was aggressive and incoherent on admission, and then she had a tonic/clonic seizure, started foaming at the mouth and lapsed into unconsciousness. She's taken something at a party, but nobody would say what.'

'Looks to me like ecstasy—MDMA,' James Slater said tightly. 'Right, let's get on this. Bloods, please. Let's find out what's going on. Have you given her anything?'

'IV diazepam. Why do they do it?' Livvy muttered, but it was a rhetorical question and, anyway, nobody had time to answer her.

He rattled off a list of tests he wanted done while Livvy got another IV line in, and he nodded.

'Good. Right, let's get some normal saline into her, please, and let's get these clothes off and cool her down before we lose her. And can someone talk to her friends, please, and find out for sure what she's taken? What's her temperature?'

'Forty point one.'

'Right, she's got malignant hyperthermia—'

'She's taken a cocktail,' Jenny said, coming back in. 'MDMA, something else, nobody knows what, all washed down with vodka, and then she's drunk lots and lots of water because someone told her to.'

'Damn. She's got dilutional hyponatraemia as well. Right, let's catheterise her quick, and get her on IV frusemide and try and shift this. And we need to alert PICU, she's going to have to go up there if we don't want to lose her.'

They didn't lose her, although it got worryingly close at one point, and finally she was shipped off to PICU for intensive care and Livvy went to talk to her parents before going home an hour late.

She crawled into bed, checked her phone and found a text from Matt.

Can we make it six tomorrow? Kids are having sleepover with my sainted mother. :)

She felt a quiver of anticipation, her exhaustion forgotten, and replied.

Sorry, vile shift, just got this but six is fine. Looking forward to it. How did you talk her into it?! x

He didn't reply, but then she didn't expect him to, not at gone midnight, but it pinged into her phone at seven the next morning.

She offered—disturbingly! It seems mothers have second sight. I'll see you in eleven hours. M x

Her whole body fizzing with anticipation, she spent the morning in the garden weeding, then cleaned the house, changed the sheets on her bed and went shopping for breakfast items and a few other things. Just in case...

And then she showered, ransacked her wardrobe and wondered what he called casual. How casual? He'd talked about jeans and a shirt, but there were a million different ways of doing that.

It was hot, too, but the pub was on the river, so there might be a cool breeze. Cropped jeans and a pretty top? A skirt? Or her ultimate go-to, a bold print jersey maxi-dress that she could dress up with chunky beads and heels, or wear with beach sandals.

'Stop overthinking it!' she told herself, and put on the dress and the minimum of make-up, left her hair down and slipped on a pair of toe-post sandals. Her toenails were still OK from the previous weekend, and she stood back and looked critically at herself.

The dress, like most of her more fitted clothes, had a bit of detail over the bust to disguise her lop-sidedness, a wrap-over with a twist in this case, and although if she lifted her arm her scar would show, he'd seen it anyway and it was time to stop hiding in the shadows and get over herself.

She stopped fussing, tidied her bedroom, grabbed a cardi in case it got chilly by the water and went downstairs to wait, her heart jiggling in her chest. Was tonight the night? Would he want to make love to her, or was it still too soon? Probably, but her reckless side, the side that wanted to live life to the full and not waste a single minute more, really, really hoped not…

CHAPTER SEVEN

SHE WAS WEARING another long dress, but casual this time, light-years away from the formal gown of last weekend, and she still looked gorgeous. More so, even, because this time he *knew* what was underneath, and he couldn't wait to see it again.

He pulled her into his arms and kissed her, massively tempted not to bother with dinner, but he wanted to do this properly, so he lifted his head reluctantly and nuzzled the tip of her nose with his.

'You've caught the sun.'

'Mmm. I spent the morning weeding the garden and getting some vitamin D.'

He chuckled and let her go. 'So, are you ready?'

'Yup—if I'm OK like this?'

He ran his eyes over her again, just for the joy of it, and smiled. 'Very OK,' he said softly, and she smiled.

'Let's go, then.'

* * *

It wasn't far to the pub, just a few miles, but he was right, the view was stunning, and the light breeze off the water made it perfect.

That, and having him sitting beside her on the terrace on a picnic bench overlooking the river. He was wearing dark jeans with a white linen shirt and deck shoes, and he looked every bit as gorgeous as he had the week before. It wasn't the tux, she decided as he put the drinks down in front of them and settled himself beside her, it was him. She caught a waft of cologne warmed by his skin, felt the brush of his thigh, the touch of his fingers as he lifted a strand of hair away from her eyes and tucked it behind her ear, and she wanted him more than she could believe was possible.

It was the first time since Mark, the first time ever since her cancer that she'd got this close to anyone, but she'd never expected to feel so much and now she was impatient.

Later, she told herself, and turned her attention to the menu, poring over it with him.

'Oh, it's too hard, it all looks delicious.'

'We can always come again.'

She smiled up at him. 'Sounds like a plan. So, what are we eating today?'

In the end they both chose the same—a crab

and prawn tian with avocado, followed by pan-fried local sea bass served on a bed of samphire with a mixed leaf salad and sweet potato fries on the side. She wouldn't normally have had the fries, but just this once she let herself indulge, and they were delicious.

All of it was, the food simple but beautifully cooked, and in between mouthfuls they talked.

Not about work. He banned that, and she was more than happy to forget about the previous evening's shift, but he told her what he'd done that day with his children, and she could see the love shining in his eyes as he talked about them affectionately.

They'd been to the beach with Ed and Annie and their children, and they'd built sandcastles and the children had buried him and Ed in the sand and then tickled their feet.

'It was great. Really good day. And no tantrums,' he said with a chuckle, as if that was a rare thing.

'Sounds like you had fun,' she said, hoping she didn't sound too wistful, and he nodded wryly.

'We did, but the beach has its downside. Any time you feel like getting all your orifices filled with sand, come and join us. I'm sure the children will oblige.'

'Gosh, you make it sound so tempting,' she said with a laugh, and it was, in a way. Not the orifices, obviously, but the rest of it, and she felt a pang of longing to be there with them, to be part of it, the chaos and laughter, the warmth, the love. Was he inviting her to join them, or was it just a throwaway remark? She wasn't sure, but maybe it was still too soon. The last thing she'd want was for his children to be hurt, but it didn't stop the longing.

'Are you going to finish your fries?' he asked, and she pulled herself together and thought about him, not his children, not her un-born babies who were just a distant dream, but him, the man. That's what this was all about, and that's all it was about, at least for now and maybe for ever.

'No, you go ahead,' she said, and pushed the plate towards him.

And then at last they were done, the food eaten, the conversation coming to a natural halt, and he turned to her, his eyes searching, and her heart skipped a beat.

'Coffee here, or home?' he asked quietly, the unspoken question hanging in the air between them, and she smiled.

'Home, I think, don't you?' she murmured.

'Sounds good to me,' he said softly. 'Don't move, I'll go and pay the bill.'

* * *

'So, your place or mine?'

'Mine,' she said without hesitation, and he nodded, as if he understood her reluctance to go back to his house with all its reminders of his wife and children.

He'd been openly affectionate and flirting with her all evening, so by the time he pulled up outside her house she was tingling with anticipation. She hoped she wasn't misreading him. She didn't think so.

She unlocked the door and he followed her in and headed for the kettle.

'Green tea?' he asked over his shoulder, and she took a deep breath and dredged up her courage.

'I'd rather undress you. I've been fantasising about it ever since I opened the door to you.'

He turned slowly towards her. 'I thought that was my line?'

'Mmm, it was, but that was last week and this is now, so I thought I'd steal it.'

His smile widened, a slow, sexy smile that flooded his eyes with promise. 'I've been shopping,' he murmured, patting his pocket, and she felt the tension ramp up, humming in the air between them.

'So have I,' she confessed, and he laughed and hugged her.

'So what are we waiting for?' he asked softly, and followed her up the stairs.

'I tidied up for you this time,' she said lightly, hoping her voice didn't reflect her nerves, and he chuckled and put his arms around her from behind, nuzzling his face against hers so she could feel the slight rasp of stubble against her cheek.

'Do you really think I care?'

'Well, I've seen your house, it's pretty tidy.'

He turned her round and dropped a kiss on the tip of her nose. 'Not guilty. I have a cleaner, and my mother tidies constantly.'

'Don't spoil it,' she teased. 'I was imagining you were highly domesticated.'

He laughed. 'Hardly. I do what's strictly necessary and I don't waste time on the things that aren't. Like small talk,' he added with that lazy, sexy smile making another appearance.

He feathered a gentle kiss over her lips, then lifted his head again, his expression changed, his eyes suddenly darker.

'You looked lovely tonight, sitting there by the river with the wind in your hair, all sunkissed and radiant and bubbling with laughter.' He brushed his knuckles lightly over her cheek. 'I want you so much. I haven't been able to think about anything else all week.'

'Me, too,' she said, and cradling his jaw in

her hand, she held his searching gaze. 'Come to bed, Matt. I need you. Make love to me,' she murmured, and he closed his eyes and turned his face into her palm, pressing his lips to it for a moment.

She could feel the slight prickle of stubble against her palm, the jump of a muscle under her fingertips, then he lifted his head and met her eyes again.

'It'll be a pleasure,' he said gruffly, his hands reaching for her, but she pushed his hands away and started to undo his shirt.

'My turn first,' she said, and unhurriedly, button by button, garment by garment, she peeled away his clothes with shaking fingers until he was standing in front of her naked.

Naked, beautiful and very, very ready.

He lifted his hand and touched her cheek, his fingers trailing slowly, slowly down over her throat, dipping under her collar bones, tracing the neckline of her dress. Her heart was hammering so hard against her ribs she thought they'd break, and she took a step back and caught hold of the dress.

'Uh-uh. My turn,' he said, and then frowned and made a face, and she laughed.

'It just pulls off,' she said, putting him out of his misery, and he laughed with her and said, 'Good,' and reaching for the dress he hitched it up slowly, his hands brushing tantalisingly against her legs. He paused to cup her bottom and ease her against himself with a quiet groan, then moved on up her body, inch by inch, past her hips, her waist, her ribs, until finally he peeled it carefully over her head and dropped it to the floor.

And then he stood there and stared down at her, his eyes lowered so she couldn't read them.

Why? Why had he stopped?

She'd expected to feel nervous, but suddenly she was more worried about him now, about what he was feeling, if it was too soon, if he was really ready for what had to be a huge psychological milestone. Hers felt monumental enough. What it was like for him? Had he changed his mind—?

No, if his next words meant anything.

'Do you remember what you said to me in Cumbria,' he murmured, his voice low, 'about you being inside your body, not me?' His finger traced a line down her throat, between her breasts, down to her abdomen, his hand flattening against her, fingers splayed across the lace of her shorts, so near and yet so far. 'It's been driving me mad ever since. It's all I can think about.'

'Well, don't let me stop you,' she said a little breathlessly, and he laughed softly and met her eyes again.

'First things first.'

He reached around behind her, sifting her hair through his fingers for a moment, then his hands moved down and he took off her underwear with gentle, careful fingers, peeling away her bra, then her lacy shorts, dropping them on their other clothes.

Then he straightened up, his eyes trailing slowly over her body before he muttered something and turned away abruptly, and she had a sudden rush of insecurity.

He picked up his trousers and her heart sank, but then he found his wallet and pulled something out, and relief swamped her.

'Oh... For a moment there, I thought you were going.'

'Going?' He gave her a quizzical smile. 'I'm not going anywhere. No way on earth. I was just getting these.'

He dropped the little foil packets on the bedside table, turned back the bedclothes and took her in his arms with a deep groan.

'Oh, that feels so good,' he said, and then his mouth found hers, slow and coaxing, his tongue delving as his hands roamed gently over her body, driving her wild. She threaded her fingers through his hair, running her other hand slowly down over his back, feeling the strong muscles that bracketed his spine, the hot silk of his skin, the contrast as her hand moved round and down over his taut abdomen.

'Livvy—!'

She heard the sharp hiss of his indrawn breath as her fingers circled him, but he didn't stop her, just slid his hand down between their bodies, his knee nudging her legs apart, his fingers gentle and sure and devastatingly accurate.

She clenched her legs together around his thigh, her legs giving way, and he scooped her up and laid her in the middle of the bed, following her down, his mouth never leaving hers. His hand found her again, coaxing, teasing, building the tension until she wanted to scream.

Then he pulled away and reached for the bedside table.

'Let me,' she said, her voice unsteady. She tore the foil wrapper open with fingers that shook a little, pushed him onto his back and straddled his thighs, stroking him teasingly with a fingertip from his collar bones all the way down, down, slowly, tantalisingly, following the narrow line of dark hair—

'Livvy, please, get on with it,' he begged, laughing a little desperately, and she obliged, slowly rolling the condom down, drawing it out deliberately even though it was killing her because she wanted him so much. She wasn't alone. He swore and grabbed the sheet, clenching it in his fists, his eyes tight shut.

'What are you doing to me?' he mumbled through gritted teeth, and she laughed.

'You know *exactly* what I'm doing to you,' she murmured, and then she moved up until she was straddling his hips, chafing against him, watching his control waver as she lowered herself slowly down over him, taking him into her body, giving it time to adjust.

He tilted his hips and she gave an involuntary gasp and rocked against him, and his eyes opened and locked with hers, his hands reaching for her, grasping her hips and holding her still.

'*Don't—move.*'

She rocked again, just gently, and he groaned.

'Livvy…'

'I'm so close…'

He rolled then, taking her with him, their bodies meshed together, legs tangled, his control splintering as he picked up the pace.

His hand slid between them again, his body shifting slightly so he could reach her, his mouth never leaving hers, and she felt the tension tighten unbearably, building until she thought she'd scream, but still she couldn't let go.

'Now, Livvy, please, come with me,' he said raggedly, and as his body stiffened she felt the tightly coiled tension inside her shatter into a million pieces.

She sobbed his name, and then as the avalanche of sensation died away he sagged against her, his head on her shoulder, his breath rasping. She could feel his heart pounding against her chest, feel the heat of his breath, the ripple of shock waves running through them both.

For the longest moment neither of them moved, and then he lifted his head and stared down into her eyes.

'Oh, Livvy,' he said, his voice catching, and he touched his mouth to hers in a tender kiss that nearly broke her heart.

He had to move.

He rolled away from her, breaking the contact reluctantly, and got to his feet, his legs barely holding him.

'Back in a moment, I need to deal with this,' he said gruffly, and headed for the bathroom, closing the door behind him and resting back against it for a second while his emotions settled.

I love her.

The thought was so profound, so over-whelming, it nearly broke him.

How? How, so soon?

In a daze, he dealt with the condom, washed his hands and face and stood staring at himself in her bathroom mirror.

Had Jules meant so little to him that he'd re-placed her this fast? Except he hadn't replaced her, not at all. He still loved her, and he knew he always would, but was it possible he loved Olivia as well?

How could that be? And it was so sudden, so unexpected.

Happiness, yes, he could buy that, but—*love?*

No. It was just the heat of the moment. It couldn't be love. Love took years to grow, to turn into that almost organic state where you could finish each other's sentences and antici-pate the other's needs and wishes.

That was love—wasn't it? Not this barely there, untried emotion that he felt for Livvy.

Well, untried, anyway. It wasn't barely there, it was very much present, and he felt as if he'd been punched in the gut.

He opened the door and went back to her and found her sitting on the edge of the bed. She looked up at him, her eyes wary.

'Are you OK?' she asked.

He found a smile. Actually, it wasn't hard. Not hard at all. 'Yes. Yes, I'm fine,' he said quietly, realising he was. 'Very fine. How are you?'

'I'm very fine, too, thank you,' she said, and her smile was tender and loving.

Her, too?

No. It was just the magic of the moment, nothing more. It couldn't be more.

'Good,' he said, as she got to her feet and came over to him and rested against him for a moment. He lifted a hand and cradled her head against his chest, and then she straightened up and smiled at him.

'I need the bathroom. I won't be long.'

He lay down again, staring blindly up at her bedroom ceiling, his thoughts tumbling.

OK, so it wasn't love, but what was it? He didn't know, and he couldn't work out what he felt.

Not regret, he knew that without a shadow of a doubt. It had been wonderful, amazing, and he'd been more than ready. What he wasn't ready for was the tidal wave of emotion that had swept over him when she'd come apart in his arms.

He heard water running, the door opening,

CAROLINE ANDERSON 173

and then she was back, snuggling down beside him and bringing warmth and joy with her.

They didn't speak. There didn't seem to be anything to say, or any need to say it.

He turned his head slightly and pressed a gentle kiss to her forehead, and she tipped her head back and smiled up at him, her lips irresistible.

He didn't even try to resist.

His kiss was gentle, unhurried, his lips lazily sipping and tasting, the urgency gone now from both of them.

He eased the bedclothes away, his hand tracing a path down her throat, down over her shoulder to her wrist, trailing over the pulse point. He lifted her hand and laid a gentle, lingering kiss on the palm, then threaded his fingers through hers and worked his way slowly back up the inside of her arm, kissing every inch.

He reached her armpit and paused before he reached the scar, lifting his head and meeting her eyes searchingly.

She felt a quiver of resistance and quelled it. This was Matt, who'd just made the most beautiful and tender love to her. She was safe with him.

'Does it feel strange? Would you rather

I didn't touch it?' he asked softly, and she shrugged.

'No, it's fine. It's numb, so it's a bit weird—but that's OK.'

He nodded, traced the scar gently with his fingers—checking out the surgery, probably, in doctor mode—then bent his head and feathered slow, tiny kisses along its length, definitely not in doctor mode now but back to the gentle, sensitive lover who seemed to know how to make her body sing, even there.

It was strangely soothing, if a bit unnerving, but then he reached the end of the scar and moved on, his tongue flicking lightly over her nipple, and she sucked in a breath and clenched her legs together as the sensation rippled through her.

'Oh—!'

He paused and lifted his head. 'Is that a good oh, or a bad oh?' he asked, and she laughed a little.

'Definitely good.'

He smiled wickedly and did it again, then treated the other breast to the same torture until she was ready to scream. And then he moved on, his stubble grazing lightly over her skin as he sipped and nibbled his way down over her ribs to her abdomen.

And then he paused and traced a fingertip

along the fine, almost invisible line that ran from side to side just above her waist.

"Whoever the surgeon was did a lovely job. Very neat.'

'It is. My father did it.'

He lifted his head and stared at her. 'Your *father*?'

'Yes. He didn't realise he was my father at the time.'

He shifted back up the bed and lay down again facing her, looking even more puzzled. 'We are talking about Oliver?'

'Of course.'

He shook his head. 'I don't understand.'

'No. He didn't, really,' she said with a smile. 'They'd had a bit of a thing at a conference a couple of years before, and they—well, whatever, he was called away in the night and he left a message to say his brother-in-law had been killed and his wife was pregnant and he had to go to her.'

His eyes widened. '*What?* Your father was *married*?'

'Sounds like it, doesn't it? Except he wasn't. It was his sister Clare's husband who was killed, and his sister who was pregnant but it all got a bit lost in the translation so when my mother realised she was pregnant she didn't tell him. Then they ended up working together at the Audley Memorial and she still thought he was married, and although he knew she had a child she still didn't tell him, and then I was rushed in after the accident without any ID, and he was on take, so he operated. He managed to save some of my spleen, repaired my bowel and flushed my abdomen and it was all going well.

'And then, just when he was about to close, he found out I was Mum's child, and he looked at me properly for the first time and realised I must be his. We share the same rare blood group, B negative, and I was the spitting image of his nephew, so he just knew.'

'Wow. So who closed? Surely not him?'

'Yes, he did. He decided he couldn't trust anybody else to do it as well as he would, because he cared more.'

Matt shook his head. 'I can't imagine operating on one of my kids. That must have been such a shock.' His finger traced the line again. 'He's done a truly beautiful job. It really doesn't show.'

'You saw it.'

He laughed and kissed her. 'I'm a surgeon, Olivia, so I do tend to notice these things. So, how was your mother about it?'

'Shocked, worried for him in case it went wrong, relieved when it didn't. She'd been about to tell him because they were seeing each other again and they were in love anyway, so they just got married pretty soon afterwards, and then Jamie and Abbie came along, and they've been nauseatingly happy ever since—or maybe that's me, being jealous because I know I'll probably never experience it.'

He frowned, his face puzzled. 'Why not?'

'Because I don't think I'll ever have my own family. I can't get pregnant while I'm on tamoxifen because it's too risky for the baby, so I'd have to wait until I come off it and allow time for it to leave my system, and by then it could be too late for my ovaries. Tamoxifen can shut them down.'

'Didn't they ask if you wanted to harvest eggs before you started treatment?'

'Yes, but it meant two months of being bombarded with hormones, my radiotherapy had already been delayed by the second op, and I was freaked out at the thought of all those missed cancer cells mopping up the hormones and invading my body, so I said no and it's haunted me ever since because that might have been my last chance, but it's done now and it's not the end of the world.'

Except sometimes it felt like it, so she tried not to think about it.

He frowned again. 'There are all sorts of

ways you can still be a mother, and it certainly shouldn't stop you being happy. You could adopt, or foster, or be a stepmother, or just be with someone without kids. Not everyone wants children, Livvy. There are lots of people who don't, for all sorts of reasons.'

'But I do,' she admitted, opening her heart to him with painful honesty and letting the sorrow seep in. 'I desperately do. I love children, all children, but that's not what it's about, and if I ended up adopting or being a stepmother I'm afraid I might resent the fact that they weren't mine, and that scares me because it wouldn't be fair to them. I just want to be pregnant, to grow a baby inside me. It's almost biological, and sometimes I just feel hollow with the need. And I don't know if I can, or if I'll ever be able to, or even if I should because of the cancer risk. And that hurts.'

'Maybe you could get pregnant once you're off tamoxifen. Women do, and surely the cancer risk is minimal now? You said they'd got it all. What stage was it?'

'Stage I, and they did get it all, and then took more tissue to be super-cautious, and I had radiotherapy and I'm taking tamoxifen, which I hate because it makes me feel rubbish—I've done everything I can, sorted my diet, my lifestyle, my priorities—so I'll almost certainly be all right, but pregnancy is years down the line. I still have hope, there's still a chance, but that's not for now and maybe not ever, because I didn't take that risk when I had the chance. It's just something I have to live with—'

Her voice cracked and she turned her head away.

'Sorry. Ignore me. I'm just having a pity party.'

'Oh, Olivia,' he whispered softly, his breath drifting over her face, and then he kissed her, tenderly now, making her eyes fill. 'I'm sorry.'

'I'm OK,' she assured him, wishing her voice sounded a bit stronger, that she hadn't shown him so much of herself, the bits she never shared, even with her parents. 'You don't need to feel sorry for me. I'm alive and well and that's enough to ask for. Alive, and making a valid contribution. I'm a good doctor, I know that, and I love it.

'And anyway, there are other things,' she went on, trying to put a positive spin on it. 'My hobbies, my family, my friends. I have a good life, Matt, and I'm fine with it most of the time. Yes, sometimes I have a bit of a wobble, but it doesn't mean I can't be happy. I'm happy now. You make me happy.'

She wasn't sure who she was trying to convince, him or herself, but his arms tightened around her, holding her closer.

'Good, because you make me happy, too,' he murmured, kissing her tenderly, and then turned out the light, wrapped her gently against his heart and held her, the steady rhythm under her ear soothing as she drifted into sleep.

He lay awake for a long time, feeling the slight rise and fall of her chest against his side, the whisper of her breath against his skin, her words running through his head in a continuous loop.

Such sad words, said in such a brave, determined voice that didn't hide the pain that lay beneath it.

I just want to be pregnant...carry a baby inside me...hollow with the need...haunted me ever since...might have been my last chance... didn't take the risk.

And then the other things she'd said, about being a stepmother.

I might resent the fact that they weren't mine and that scares me...it wouldn't be fair to them.

He'd thought it himself, thought as he'd lain awake in the middle of the night all last week that his priority had to be to keep his relationship with her and his children separate, to keep them apart from each other until he knew where this was going so there was no chance of his children being hurt or confused, but that was before he realised he loved her, before he realised he wanted more. Much, much more.

Well, Juliet's death had taught him that you didn't always get what you wanted, you got the hand life dealt you, and if the hand he'd been dealt meant he could share only a small area of his life with her, would that be so bad?

They could still be together, still be happy, just not all the time. And if they managed that right, made sure they made time for each other regularly, then maybe that would be enough, for both of them, until they were sure of each other. And maybe then, if she met his children, maybe she'd realise that she wouldn't resent them. Maybe they could become her family?

No. He was getting ahead of himself. It was much too soon to start thinking about things like that.

Wasn't it?

Carefully, so he didn't wake her, he eased his arm out from under her head and shifted slightly away, throwing off the covers. It was a hot night, and he needed air.

Trying not to disturb her, he got quietly out of bed, picked up his jeans and underwear and went downstairs, letting himself out into the garden.

The moon was full, and he sat on her swinging bench at the top of the little paved garden and inhaled the heady fragrance of the wisteria growing over the trellis behind him. It reminded him of Jules, of the night-scented stocks she'd planted in amongst the shrubs just before she'd died, but suddenly it all seemed a long, long time ago, and his life was in the here and now.

With Livvy? He hoped so.

But what about the children? They'd gain so much from her being a part of their lives, and they had so much to give her, but was it fair to expect it from either them or her? And what if she *did* resent them?

No. There was no way she'd do anything other than love them with her whole heart and soul. She didn't have a resentful, selfish bone in her body, he was sure of it. He just had to prove it to her.

He breathed in again, drawing in the scent, letting it fill his lungs. It was beautiful, the silence of the night broken only by the sound of a distant siren and the faint creak of the chains as the bench swung slowly back and forth, and he closed his eyes and let the peace soak into him, but even so his mind couldn't rest and his heart ached for her.

Why did life have to be so complicated?

CHAPTER EIGHT

HE'D GONE.

She hadn't heard anything, no doors closing, no car starting, but there was a silent quality about the house that told her she was alone, and she wanted to cry.

She wished she'd kept her mouth shut. No doubt it had made him realise he should protect his children from her, just in case.

They'd never discussed her meeting Amber and Charlie, and if she was honest she wasn't sure she wanted to, maybe because she'd want it too much, or because she was afraid she'd be resentful of his happiness, but maybe that was irrelevant if he'd decided their relationship couldn't go anywhere further because of the children.

Not that he'd said anything that in any way implied he *wanted* it to go further, and it was far too soon even to think about it, but what if, now he knew she probably couldn't have children, he'd thought she only wanted him because of his ready-made family, a substitute for the babies she could never have?

Had he doubted her motives? She hoped not, because she really didn't have any apart from wanting to be with him. But his children had to come first, and if he'd had the slightest shred of doubt, he had a duty to protect them. She understood that absolutely, but it hurt that he might believe she'd use him—use all of them—like that.

Yes, her heart ached to be part of a noisy, busy family, but she didn't know how she'd feel about someone else's children, if she'd be happy or if they'd just constantly remind her of what she'd missed out on. She hadn't even let herself think about his children, just to make it easier, but she was sure he must have done. They'd suffered enough—and so had she. There was no point torturing herself unnecessarily.

She laughed at that. Torturing herself? What was she thinking? It was him she'd tortured, burdening him with her self-pity, and she felt a rush of guilt.

At least she was alive. She thought about the woman with dark hair who would never see her babies grow up, about the pictures they'd drawn, scattered like confetti over his fridge and the playroom walls, the people who were alive now because of his generosity in donating her organs.

She thought about the life he lived without her, a juggling act between work and home, with his indispensable mother filling in the gaps and having the children for a sleepover so he could have a life, even if it was only one night in however many that he could snatch off from reality.

And she felt sorry for *herself*?

She was flooded with shame, disgusted at her neediness when he needed her far more than she needed him. She was fine. She had a great life. He didn't, not any more, because it had all been snatched unfairly from him when Jules had died. And if sharing her life with him could bring him a crumb of happiness, a fleeting moment of downtime from responsibility on the rare occasions when he could get away, then she would do it without question.

She wanted more of him than that, much more, but she knew she couldn't have it, knew he wasn't ready for it, and if that was all they could ever have she'd take it willingly, because she'd rather have that occasional little glimpse of paradise with him than the drab grey of life without him.

Except now he'd gone, and she didn't know

why. Maybe it *was* because of the children, or maybe it was simply that common sense had reared its ugly head and he'd run for cover from a broken, needy woman who didn't know how to keep her mouth shut.

Wise man.

Disgusted with herself, she threw off the bedclothes, pulled on her dressing gown and padded downstairs, and then she realised the back door was open. And she could hear a sound, a familiar, rhythmic creak.

She walked silently into the conservatory and there he was at the top of her little garden, his eyes closed, head tilted back, one foot pushing the bench. Push, swing, push, swing.

He hadn't gone...

She walked up to him, her feet almost silent on the paving, but she must have made a sound because his eyes opened and he smiled and held out a hand to her and pulled her gently onto his lap.

'I'm sorry, I just felt like some fresh air. Did I wake you?'

She shook her head, relief flooding her.

'No, I was just hot—the joys of tamoxifen. Are you OK?'

He smiled again, his eyes unreadable, shadowed in the stark light of the moon, and she felt his thigh tense as he gave the ground another little push, rocking the swing again.

'Yeah, I'm fine. You?'

She nodded. 'I thought you'd gone because of my self-pitying little misery fest.'

He laughed softly and hugged her closer. 'No. I'm still here. You don't get rid of me that easily. Your garden smells amazing at night, by the way. I love it. I wish mine was like this.'

'Give yours time. I'm sure you've got some wonderful plants in there.'

She rested her head against his and closed her eyes, relishing the feel of his bare chest under her hand, the rhythmic shift of his thighs as he rocked the swing, his solid warmth, his gentleness, his strength. She was so glad he hadn't gone, but he'd have to soon, and she wasn't ready for that. Not yet.

'What time are you picking up the children?'

'I'm not. My mother said she'd keep them till lunch if I wanted. She'll probably take them to the beach. Why?'

'I just wondered how long we've got.'

He tilted his head back and looked up at her, his smile sad. 'Not nearly long enough.'

She bent her head and kissed him tenderly, needing to feel his arms around her, his body close to hers because that might be all she could ever have of him.

'Then let's not waste it,' she murmured, and pulled him to his feet and took him back to bed.

His phone pinged at eight, and he reached out for it, then put it down and pulled her back into his arms with a contented little noise.

'Everything OK?'

'Mmm, it's fine. It was Mum. They're off to the beach with Ed and Annie and all the children before it gets too hot.'

She felt a pang of guilt for keeping him from his little family. 'Shouldn't you go? Your time with them's so limited.'

He tilted his head back so he could look at her, his eyes searching. 'Do you want me to go?'

'No! Well—only if you want to. I just don't want you to feel you have to stay. You see little enough of them, and they're only small and they need you. You should go, really.'

'You're right.' He smiled, kissed her and rolled out of bed, straightening up with a bone-cracking stretch. 'Let's go to mine for breakfast, and then we can wander down to the beach and join up with them later.'

'Really?'

He sat back down on the edge of the bed and took her hand. 'Really. I think it's time you met my children,' he said seriously, and she felt her eyes widen, her heart suddenly beating just that little bit faster.

'Are you sure?' she asked, feeling a little stunned, a little panicked because she'd been sure he'd never let her near them after all she'd said.

'They don't bite,' he said gently, but that wasn't what she was worried about. It was more the possibility that having met them she'd love them instantly, as part of him, and she wasn't sure she wanted to expose herself to that much hurt in case their relationship didn't last.

'Don't you want to keep us apart?'

'No. It's fine.' His smile was warm and a little wry. 'Don't worry, I won't tell them what we've been up to.'

'I didn't think you would for a moment, but what *will* you tell them? And how about your mother? What will she think?'

'She won't think anything. She knows we're together, it was her idea, and they're my children and I'd like you to meet them, unless you really, really don't want to. I'll just tell them you're my friend from work. They already know a bit about you.'

She felt her eyes pop open wider still. 'They do?'

He laughed softly. 'Yes, they do. I told them

about you falling down the mountain. Amber was walking along a low garden wall, and it was getting higher and higher as the road went down the hill, and I told her to be careful and she said, "Daddy, I'm *always* careful!", which sounded so like you. So I told them about you.'

She bit her lip, trying not to laugh and failing. 'I can't believe you told them. They'll think I'm an idiot.'

'Oh, well, if the cap fits—'

'You're so rude,' she said, swatting him playfully and laughing, but he just hugged her.

'Don't worry about them, they don't judge, they're just small people. They take everything at face value. And I know my mother would like to meet you.'

To see if she measured up? She chewed her lip, the laughter vanishing in an instant. 'It's not that I don't want to meet them all, I do—'

'Well, that's all right, then,' he said firmly, and twitched the covers off her. 'Come on, gorgeous. Let's hit the shower.'

'Together?'

He grinned and pulled her to her feet. 'Why not?'

He hustled her through the shower, keeping it brisk and matter-of-fact in the end because otherwise they'd get sidetracked and he wanted to get home now and get on with the day.

Starting with breakfast, and then going to the beach.

They took the food she'd bought back to his house, made a stack of club sandwiches and ate them on his bench while she ran a critical eye over the new shrubs and the ones that had been hacked back.

'I think you just need to be patient,' she said. 'You've got some beautiful things.'

He laughed and shook his head. 'How would I know? I can recognise wisteria and roses. Beyond that, I'm useless.'

'My mother loves gardening, she taught me everything I know. Come on, let's have a look,' she coaxed, and gave him a guided tour of his own garden, pointing out the names of each of the shrubs she recognised, their various merits and flowering season, and after a while he was convinced she was stalling.

Well, he wasn't going to let her, wasn't going to give her any further opportunity to try and talk both of them out of going to the beach so she could meet the children. He'd been thinking about it all night because he knew that until he saw them together, until he saw her reaction to his children and theirs to her, he had no idea what the future might hold for them all, and he needed to know.

And so did she.

She was telling him about the *viburnum tinus* which had been cut back hard when he stopped her in mid-flow, a finger on her lips.

'Enough,' he said, laughing down into her eyes. 'We can do this another time. Let's go to the beach, it's less challenging.'

Really?

Maybe for him, but not for her, which was why she'd been stalling furiously.

By the time they'd crossed the road, gone down the ramp to the slipway and walked along to the Shackletons' beach hut, her heart was thrashing in her chest. What would the children think of her? Would they hate her? And would she, as she feared, fall instantly in love with them both? What if she didn't? What if she resented them? If they resented her?

He was walking beside her but a careful distance away, not quite touching, and all of a sudden there was a flurry of arms and legs and a little girl with their mother's dark hair hurled herself at him.

'Daddy!'

'Hello, my little princess!'

He swung her up and round, his laugh echoing through her, and she felt a huge lump in her throat seeing them together, their obvious joy in each other, the love that shone from both their faces. He put her back on her feet and scooped up a boy, smaller than Amber but the spitting image of his mother except for his father's smile.

The lump in her throat got even bigger as she watched him hug and kiss his grubby, sandy little son, and when he put him back down on the ground and turned to her, she had to struggle to find a smile.

'Livvy, meet my children, Amber and Charlie. Guys, this is Olivia, my friend from work. Say hello.'

'Hello, Amber, hello, Charlie.'

In typical little-boy fashion Charlie mumbled what could have been hello and ran off, distracted by two small boys about a year younger than him, probably Ed and Annie's twins. She turned back to Amber, who was studying her seriously.

'Are you the lady who fell down the mountain?'

Livvy bit her lip and tried not to laugh, but it was hopeless. 'Your daddy's been telling tales,' she said, and Amber shook her head, all serious still.

'He told me you were being silly, just like I

was on the wall, and you could have hurt your-self a lot worse.'

Her smile faded. 'Yes, I could have done. He's quite right. And he did warn me, and I stupidly didn't listen.'

She nodded sagely. 'He said that, too,' she said, deadpan, and Livvy had to bite the inside of her cheeks. 'Is your ankle better now?'

'Yes, thank you. It's fine now.'

Amber nodded and cocked her head on one side. 'I like your dress, it's very pretty.'

She'd pulled on the jungle-print dress she'd worn the night before, just for speed and because it was so easy to wear—and, to be honest, because he'd told her she looked beautiful when she was wearing it, and that made her feel beautiful.

'I'm glad you like it. It's my favourite dress.'

'My favourite dress doesn't really fit me any more and Daddy says I need a new one, but he hates shopping,' Amber said sadly.

There was a snort from beside her, and she looked up to see Matt rolling his eyes and laughing. 'I don't hate it, but I am hopeless. Hopeless and completely out of my depth.'

'And Grandma hates it, too, and Daddy says she's always buying things and taking them back because she can't make up her mind. And Auntie Sally's too busy, and I haven't got a mummy any more,' she added, and Livvy sucked in a quiet breath.

'I could take you,' she said before she engaged her filter, and Amber's eyes widened in excitement.

'Really? That would be amazing!'

'Well, that's me off the hook,' Matt said lightly, but his smile spoke volumes and she just hoped he didn't read too much into it.

There wasn't time to speculate, though, because Amber slipped her warm, sandy hand into Livvy's and dragged her over to a group of women clustered round the front of a beach hut.

'Grandma, this is Daddy's friend Olivia,' she said importantly, that little hand still holding hers, 'and she's going to take me shopping for a new favourite dress.'

Four pairs of eyes locked onto her, and not for the first time today she wished she'd kept her mouth shut...

'Oh, that's nice, Amber,' one of them said, getting to her feet. 'How kind of her. Matt, darling, why don't you and Amber go and help Ed with the children? We'll be fine.'

He shrugged, held his hand out to Amber and left her there feeling slightly abandoned and with a definite case of interview nerves.

'Hello, Olivia. I'm Jane, Matt's mother,' the woman said, giving her a slightly sandy handshake and a warm smile. 'It's lovely to meet you at last. Let me introduce you to Marnie, Ed's grandmother, and Joanna, Annie's mother, and Annie who's married to Ed, but of course you know that. And those are their four children on the beach.'

They all greeted her with friendly smiles and welcoming words, but she could see the questions lined up in their eyes.

She glanced across to where Ed and the girls were helping the little ones build a sandcastle, but Matt had his back to her and was clearly not going to be any help at all, and as he reached them Ed lifted his hand and waved at her.

'Hi, Livvy. How's it going?' he called.

She wasn't answering that loaded question under any circumstances, so she just smiled, said, 'Good, thanks,' and turned back to the women, leaving him and Matt to it. She had enough on her plate dodging the bullets she felt were coming her way any minute.

'What a lovely beach hut,' she said, casting about for something neutral, and Annie picked it up seamlessly.

'Yes, it's amazing. It belongs to Marnie but we sort of share it. So, it's lovely to meet you at last. How's the ankle?' she asked, bringing the conversation neatly back to her, and she laughed and rolled her eyes.

'I'm never going to live that down, am I?' she said, and Matt's mother and Annie both shook their heads and laughed with her.

'I was just about to make some drinks. Tea or coffee?' Annie asked, heading for the beach hut's tiny kitchen area, and Livvy followed her as the safest bet.

'I don't really drink either, I'm afraid, unless you have decaf? Or fruit tea?'

'There's a really nice peppermint green tea?'

'Perfect,' she said, and Annie put the kettle on and smiled at her thoughtfully.

Here we go.

'So, you're the person who's put the smile back on Matt's face. I'm so pleased. It's great to see him looking happy again.'

That surprised her. 'I thought Ed didn't approve?'

Annie frowned slightly. 'I don't think it was that. He was worried—about you getting hurt, and Matt getting in deeper than he was ready for. They've been friends for years, ever since they were at school, and he was just worried about him. It's been really tough for him.'

She nodded slowly. 'I know. I knew they were friends, that was obvious, but I didn't realise they went back that far. It sort of explains—well, quite a bit, really. Matt often talks about doing things with you all, but I thought he'd only known Ed since he started at the hospital.'

'Oh, no, since they were both sixteen. They did the same science subjects, and they spent a lot of time together, apparently. I'm so glad he came back here when the job came up. Jane's really been through the mill, too, what with losing her husband to cancer and then supporting Matt after Jules died, and it's been a really positive move for all of them, I think, after such a run of tragedies.'

His father had died of cancer? Oh, no...

Annie straightened up and smiled. 'Still, that's all in the past now, and he's got something to look forward to.'

'I think it's a little soon to assume that,' she said quickly, trying to cut off the matchmaking look in Annie's eyes before it took hold too firmly, but Annie just smiled.

'Well, we'll just have to wait and see,' she murmured, but then the kettle whistled, to Livvy's relief, and Annie turned off the gas, reached for some mugs and made everyone a drink, and—for now at least—she was off the hook.

It was warming up to be a scorching hot day, and by eleven o'clock they'd packed everything up and were heading back towards the clifftop.

'We're having a barbecue,' Ed said, falling into step beside them as they got to the top. 'Want to come?'

'Yeah, that would be great,' Matt said. 'Livvy?'

'Yes, Olivia, please, *please* come?' Amber squealed, and she looked at Ed.

'Did you mean me, too?'

'Well, yes, of course,' Ed said, as if it was a foregone conclusion that she'd be coming if they did. 'Unless you don't want to come?'

'No, I— That would be lovely, but you won't have catered for me.'

He laughed as if she'd said something hilarious. 'We don't cater, Livvy. We throw stuff on the barbecue until people stop eating. You'll be fine.'

'Matt?'

'Yes. Absolutely, yes.'

'Well, in that case—thank you, that would be lovely.'

Amber squealed again and grabbed her hand, bouncing up and down on the end of her arm like a yo-yo, and she had to laugh, but deep in the pit of her stomach was lodged a nugget of fear that meeting all these lovely people had been a huge, huge mistake, one she might well regret for the rest of her life.

* * *

She was sitting on the grass in the cool, dappled shade of a birch tree, the leaves whispering in the light breeze coming off the sea, and Annie wandered over and sat beside her, snatching a moment of peace.

She'd brought cold drinks with her, and Livvy took hers and sat back with a sigh.

'Thank you. This shade is just lovely.'

'It is, isn't it? So, how are you getting on in the ED? I still miss it in a way, but I wouldn't trade it for the world.'

She laughed, hoping it didn't sound too hollow. 'I can understand that. Why swap your children for the ritual abuse of a Friday night?'

Annie chuckled. 'I have to say I don't miss that at all. I don't remember a single one that wasn't hideous.'

'No, last Friday was awful,' she said. 'We had a girl who'd taken ecstasy. She's alive, but she's still in PICU and her parents are beside themselves.' She looked across at Annie thoughtfully. 'So, on the subject of daughters, since you have two, any idea where I can take Amber for a new favourite dress?'

Annie frowned. 'I imagine we're talking party dress here?'

'I have no idea. Probably.'

'There's a little boutique near the seafront

that has a children's section. It just depends how special, but they aren't outrageous and they have some lovely stuff. I've bought things for Grace and Chloe, and Kate got her wedding dress there when she and Sam got married. Have you met Kate?'

She shook her head. 'No. I'm not a mum,' she said, stifling the little pang, 'so I don't mix in the same circles. I'm just a lowly registrar with a very full-time job.'

Annie gave her an odd look. 'You don't need to be a mum, Livvy. We're all still ourselves.'

Which was all very well, but since the entire day from the moment they'd hit the beach had been all about the children, she'd felt slightly marginalised. Not that anyone had been anything but lovely to her but, still, she felt as if she didn't quite belong—

'Look out!'

She glanced up, saw the ball heading for her and lifted her arms to catch it and throw it back.

'Nice save,' Matt said with a laugh, and kicked it back towards the children.

'It's lovely to see them all together,' she said wistfully. 'You and Ed are very lucky. How long have you been together?'

'Five years?'

'But—the girls…'

'They aren't his—although you'd never know. He adores them, and he's a brilliant step-dad. Their biological father doesn't even know they exist, and frankly that's a good thing, because they don't need him. Ed's a better father than he could ever be.'

Livvy looked across the garden to where Ed and Matt were playing football with the children. So Ed was a stepfather, as well as a father, and that was obviously a huge success, but then they'd had their own children, too. If she'd had the sense to harvest some eggs, maybe she and Matt could have been in the same situation, and she could have helped him to bring up his children and her own. Not that she'd be a better mother than Jules, of course not, but she'd have given it everything she had—

But it wasn't going to happen, and there was no point wallowing in it. She'd done enough of that in the last twenty-four hours.

She pulled up a bit of grass and fiddled with it for a moment, then looked up and saw Annie watching her thoughtfully.

'So—where do you and Matt go from here?'

She shrugged. 'Nowhere, really. I'm just taking every day as it comes, and if Matt's in my life for a while that's amazing, and if not, well, I'm sure I'll cope.'

'But he loves you,' Annie said softly, her voice shocked.

She stared at her. 'No, he doesn't.'

'Yes, he does. Of course he does! Haven't you noticed the way he looks at you?'

She felt her eyes fill, and looked away. 'He doesn't love me, Annie. He's still in love with Jules. He always will be. He's just taking the edge off his loneliness, but that's fine. I know that, and so am I.'

She got to her feet, brushing the little bits of grass off her dress and slipping her feet back into her shoes. 'It's time I was going. I've got stuff to do before tomorrow, and I'm on an early shift. Thank you for a lovely day. It's been really nice to meet you.'

Annie stood up and hugged her. 'You, too. And anytime you fancy a coffee or a chat, just come and find me. I'm always around. Maybe you and Matt could come for a meal one evening. Or we could get my mother to babysit and come to you and bring the food. That might be better. I know Matt feels guilty for relying on his mother, and I've got the T-shirt for that one, too, so—whatever, talk to him and come up with a date.'

'But I—'

'Come up with a date for what?'

Matt's arm settled round her shoulders, easing her up against his side as if it was the most natural thing in the world.

Did he love her? Really?

'I've invited you both for a meal,' Annie was saying. 'Whenever you like. Are you giving Livvy a lift home? You can leave the children here, if you like.'

He met her eyes, his thoughtful. 'I was going to suggest you come back with us. The kids could do with a shower to get the sand off, but then Amber's desperate to talk dresses with you. I think she'd like to show you her wardrobe, but I can take you home if you'd rather.'

It was the Amber thing that did it.

Not the warmth of his body against hers, the tender look, the open invitation in his eyes.

Just Amber, a little girl who didn't have a mummy any more.

She'd made her a promise, and she couldn't back out now, even if she did feel a sudden and almost overwhelming urge to escape from all the cosy domesticity and get her defences back in place.

'OK. Just for a little while, then. I can always walk home, it's not far.'

CHAPTER NINE

THE 'LITTLE WHILE' stretched on into the evening, ending with them sitting on the balcony outside his bedroom, sipping ice-cold fizzy water and staring out over the sea.

'Good day?' he asked softly, and she nodded.

'Lovely day,' she said, and it had been, even if it had left an ache of longing in its wake.

'Amber's so excited about you taking her shopping. Are you sure you can cope with it?'

That made her chuckle. 'She's not quite five, Matt. I think we'll be fine. And she's absolutely right, her favourite dress is very beautiful.'

'It's a bit too beautiful, really. She can't wear it nearly as often as she'd like to. If you could find something a bit more practical but just as lovely, then she could get more use out of it.'

'I'll see what we can find. And I'll make sure it's got room for growth.'

'Oh, yes, please, so we don't have to do this again for *years*!' he said with a laugh.

'I can't promise years, Matt, that's unrealistic, but I'll do my best. Annie suggested a little boutique down by the prom. I'll track it down and have a look before I take her.'

He shifted round and studied her thoughtfully. 'You're taking this very seriously.'

'Of course I am. A pretty dress is a *serious thing*, Matt,' she said lightly. 'Ask your daughter.'

His lips twitched. 'No, thank you. I'm in enough trouble for my inability to understand as it is. Frankly, you're welcome to the job.' He reached out and took her hand, touching it to his lips, his voice suddenly serious. 'Thank you for today. I'm sure you had much better things to do than hang out with a bunch of rowdy children.'

'No, I didn't,' she said honestly, because how could she lie to him? There was nothing she'd needed to do, nothing that wouldn't wait. Well, her laundry, but that was a perennial problem and one she could deal with when she got home.

His grip on her hand tightened in a gentle squeeze. 'It's getting chilly out here. Let's go and lie on the bed,' he murmured.

'We can't!'

He smiled. 'Yeah, we can. We can still see the sea, and it's just a bit more private.'

She didn't want to. Not really, not under the eyes of Jules, watching from the top of the chest of drawers, but they went back inside and it wasn't there.

'It's gone,' she said, staring at the space where it had been, and Matt nodded.

'Yes. It's in the playroom, on the wall. I decided Amber needed to see it more than I did, and I'd stopped talking to it—to her. I used to tell her everything, ask her how to cope with stuff, and I realised I've stopped doing that now, because if I want to talk to someone, I talk to you. There'll always be a bit of me that belongs to her, but it's getting smaller every day, and there's another bit of me that I didn't even know existed that you seem to have claimed. I don't know quite how it happened, or when, but it has.'

His smile was tender, and he drew her into his arms and kissed her, just a simple, gentle kiss that made her eyes well with tears.

They lay down, and she snuggled into his side and lay staring out through the huge wall of glass, her eyes unfocused, her thoughts tracking back to last night and her fears.

'Will you tell me something honestly?' she said quietly.

'Yes, of course I will. What is it?'

'You don't think I'm only interested in you because you've got children, do you?'

For a moment he didn't speak and her heart nearly stopped, but then he sighed softly and pressed his lips to her hair.

'No. No, I don't. It did cross my mind for a moment last night, but then I thought about it, and it's just not you. You're much too considerate of others, much too thoughtful and caring—so, no, I don't think you want me for my children, because you're not a user. And besides, I practically had to drag you down to the beach to meet them, so if anything I was more worried that you *didn't* want them, but then when I saw you with Amber I stopped worrying about it.'

She shrugged. 'How could I not want them? They're lovely children. They're a real credit to you.'

He gave a soft laugh. 'I can't take any credit for that. It's been a joint effort, we've all muddled through somehow, and I'm just happy we seem to have come out of it as well as we have. And this cuts both ways, you know. You could be thinking that the only interest I have in you is that my children would benefit hugely from having a mother, because they would, of course. And I know they've got my mother and Juliet's sister, but it's not the same.'

'No. No, I don't suppose it is, and I'm sure you're right, they would benefit from a mother figure, but it won't be me.'

'Why won't it?'

His question was softly voiced, reaching down into the heart of her pain. She turned her head and met his eyes, sure he'd see the sadness that must be lurking in hers.

'It's too soon for you, and anyway I'm not a good choice, Matt. You should find someone else.'

'Maybe I don't want someone else. Maybe I want you.'

'No, you don't, you just want company. And besides, I still haven't been signed off by the oncology team and the breast surgeon.'

'Stop worrying about your cancer. It was stage I, and it's unlikely to come back, and even if it does, they can do far more for cancer now, and new advances are being made every day. And anyway, I take it you're still having regular screening?'

'Yes, and I will do for a while, I guess. I've got a mammogram in a week and a bit, and then hopefully the oncology team will sign me off and I'll be done, apart from the yearly mammograms, but there's still the joy of another five years of tamoxifen, just to be on the safe side, so even if I decided then that I wanted children, I probably couldn't have them because I'd been on it too long, so you'll never be able to have any more with me, and you might want to, so you should be with someone who can give them to you. You're a natural father—'

'Why would I need more children? I'm more than happy with my two. If I had none, I'd still want you. It's not about the children. It's about us. And you still haven't answered my question.'

'What question?'

'Do you think I'm only interested in you as a mother for my children?'

She stared at him, a little stunned because it had never occurred to her. 'No. No, of course not! I think you're lonely, and we're attracted to each other and I fill a void in your life.'

'You do more than that for me. Much more.'

'No,' she said, her voice gentle but firm. 'No, Matt, I don't, and I can't.'

She looked away, unable to hold his intense gaze. 'I need to go home. It's getting dark.'

She climbed off the bed and he followed her, his bare feet silent as they went down the stairs.

'Let me call you a taxi. I don't like the idea of you walking home alone.'

'Matt, I'll be fine.'

'Yes, you will, because you're going in a taxi.' He pulled out his phone and ordered one, then turned her gently into his arms.

'You mean so much more to me than just filling a void, Livvy,' he said softly. 'Much, much more. I—'

She pressed a finger to his lips and broke away before he could say any more, needing to get away from him because she needed him so much, wanted what he was dangling in front of her so badly that it was a physical ache, and she was sure his next words would have been 'I love you'. And that she really, really didn't want to hear. Not now, with her five-year check hanging over her.

'I'll wait outside for the taxi,' she said, pulling the door open and stepping out, her sandals in her hand, bag over her shoulder, and he sighed and followed her, sitting beside her on the garden wall as they waited for the taxi to come.

'Olivia, don't shut me out.'

'I'm not,' she lied. 'I just don't want to be any more than that to you. I don't want it to get any deeper, I don't want any expectations or promises or talk of the future. I can't deal with it. One day at a time, Matt. That's all. That's all it can ever be.'

He didn't say anything, but she could feel the tension coming off him in waves, and she heaved a silent sigh of relief when the taxi drew up.

He leant through the window, gave the taxi driver her address and paid him before he had a chance to stop her, and then closed the door behind her, his hand lifted in a silent farewell.

As the taxi pulled away, she'd never felt so lonely in her life...

Why? Why was she shutting him out?

He felt an ache in the centre of his chest, an ache he hadn't felt for two years.

Stupid. She hadn't died, she'd just told him she didn't want him as much as he'd hoped, as much as he wanted her. But it didn't add up. None of it added up. She was backing away from him, and at the same time she'd promised Amber she'd help her choose a dress, and she'd spent ages with her, delving through her clothes. He'd heard them talking and laughing in her bedroom, and when he'd looked in they'd been sitting on the floor in a pile of clothes, sorting through them, and they were both smiling.

Why do that? Why lead Amber on if she

didn't want to be part of their lives? Why lead him on?

Except she hadn't, and he'd all but dragged her to the beach today. She hadn't wanted to go, and now Amber was looking starry-eyed and it was all going to end in tears.

He swore, silently and viciously, and for the first time in ages he opened a bottle of wine, poured himself a hefty glass and went into the playroom.

Jules was looking down at him, her smile ripping a hole in his heart, and he walked out, went up to his bedroom and was instantly surrounded by Livvy, her scent lingering in the air.

He went out onto the balcony and sat down, just to get away from the reminders of the woman who'd said she didn't want him.

No. She hadn't said that. She'd said she didn't want to talk about the future. She wanted to take it one day at a time.

That's all it can ever be.

Could he do that? Take it literally one day at a time, never looking ahead, never allowing himself to dream?

He gave a hollow laugh, because it was so far from what he wanted that it was almost funny.

Didn't really have a choice, though, did he,

not the way she'd left it? But that was fine. One day at a time, he'd woo her, show her how good it could be, tell her without words how much he loved her, and hopefully he'd win her round, convince her that it would be OK, that there were no certainties in life and you couldn't live in a vacuum just waiting for the axe to fall, you had to get on with it and grab life while you had the chance.

And Amber? Should he let Livvy take her shopping, or should he protect his vulnerable little daughter from any further potential hurt? It was OK for him to take the risk, but his daughter? A tiny part of him, instantly crushed, thought that she would make a brilliant secret weapon, a way to break down Livvy's defences and let them all into her heart, but that was unfair on Amber, unfair on Livvy and so morally corrupt it sickened him that he'd even thought it.

His eyes prickled, and he tipped the wine over the balcony, went back into the bedroom and lay down, resting his head against the stack of pillows where they'd talked about the future that they'd never have.

Well, he'd see about that. It would be tough, but he'd do it. He'd done tough, he understood it, and one thing he wasn't was a quitter.

One day at a time…

* * *

She got up at the crack of dawn on Monday morning for her early shift, had a brisk shower and gave herself an even brisker talking-to.

She'd cried half the night, and her eyes were puffy, the whites reddened, and she looked like death warmed up.

She couldn't even blame it on the heat, because it had been cooler overnight, but she could hide it with make-up. Not enough to make it obvious, just enough to take the edge off, and she'd caught the sun so hopefully that would help, too.

Apparently not. Sam took one look at her and raised an eyebrow.

'Heavy night?'

'Ha-ha,' she said. 'I didn't sleep well. So, what's the plan?'

'You're in Resus with me. A car's gone off the road and the driver's impaled on some fencing. If they get him in, we'll need Matt down here, so he's on standby and we've alerted the blood bank. In the meantime, there's a patient who was brought in earlier with a drug overdose who needs monitoring. We're waiting for a bed for him. Otherwise it's quiet.'

'OK,' she said, although it was far from OK because Matt was the last person she wanted to see and for once she wished she hadn't been put in Resus. A nice little day in cubicles would have suited her fine.

In the event, Matt didn't come down, because the man impaled on fencing died at the scene from massive blood loss, so she was spared the ordeal of being professional when all she really wanted to do was throw herself into his arms and cry her eyes out and tell him she'd lied, she did want him, she wanted him desperately.

No! Stop it!

Somehow she got through the day, and she only had another hour till the end of her shift when the PA burst into life. 'Adult trauma call, ten minutes.'

Please, not soft-tissue injuries.

It was, of course. She went to Resus, and Sam briefed the team.

'OK, this is a woman in her thirties, she's fallen out of an upstairs window through the glass roof of a lean-to greenhouse, so multiple injuries and blood loss. She was stabilised at the scene, but we're going to need X-rays to trace all the glass, possibly a CT scan if we can get her stable enough, and she's going to need a lot of soft-tissue work, so I've alerted Matt Hunter, he's on his way down now, and I've got the blood bank on standby and we may need to involve Plastics, too.

'But number one, nobody pull out any glass unless it's obviously very superficial, because we don't want her suddenly bleeding out, and you all need to double-glove and be very careful of the glass splinters. She could be covered in them.'

He went through the team, allocating tasks, and then the paramedics wheeled her in and did the handover.

'This is Sarah Field, thirty-two years old, fallen through a window and landed on her right side on a glass roof and through it onto greenhouse staging. GCS fourteen at the scene, now fifteen, BP one ten over sixty-five, sats ninety-eight per cent...'

She tried to concentrate, but at the front of her mind was Matt, arriving any moment now.

How would he be with her? Distant? Wary?

Professional. Of course he was. He didn't look at her, just at the patient, most particularly her right arm, which was covered with a large pressure dressing.

She was lying on her left side, the least damaged side, and he went round and introduced himself to her, scanning her body quickly as he did so before lifting the dressing off her arm where the glass had sliced a huge flap of skin and muscle almost off.

218 A SINGLE DAD TO HEAL HER HEART

'I need to take this first, is that OK?' he asked, and Sam nodded.

'We'll work our way round the rest,' Sam said, and looked up at her. 'Livvy, can you take her head and face, please?'

Which put her right next to Matt. Tough. She ignored him, and bent over so the woman could see her.

'Hello, Sarah, my name is Olivia, I'm a doctor. Is it OK if I have a look at your face? There are some little bits of glass that I can lift out, and we need to clean off the some of the little splinters that are on the surface and then we can get a better look at you.'

'OK,' she said weakly, and Livvy started work, carefully lifting away all the visible glass fragments. A nurse was doing the same thing on her neck and shoulder, another working through her hair with a very fine comb, and her clothes were carefully cut away to expose multiple small lacerations.

'There's a flap here on her scalp,' the nurse said, and Livvy leant over at the same time as Matt, and their heads brushed.

He glanced at her, his eyes neutral. 'Sorry—may I?'

She pulled back, leaving it to him, and he issued some instructions and returned to the arm, giving her back her space.

* * *

It took nearly an hour, but finally the splinters were out, the wounds were stitched or steri-stripped or glued, and Matt had reattached the blood supply to the flap on her arm, dealt with several other wounds including the scalp flap, and was ready to take her to Theatre to start the delicate reconstruction of her arm muscles.

And finally, after all that time, he looked up and met her eyes.

'Good job on her face,' he murmured. 'Well done.'

She felt a strange little burst of pride, and smiled. 'Thank you. Good luck with the arm. I have no idea how you'll deal with such a huge flap.'

'Want to find out?'

She stared at him. 'What—in Theatre?'

'Why not? You must be about to go off, I know you were on an early, and you're interested, you said you aren't sure if surgery is for you—scrub in and find out. You can assist.'

'But I—'

'But nothing. Come on, I don't want to hang about. Are you in or out?'

'In,' she said, unconvinced about the wisdom of it but fascinated about the surgery, and in the end she was glad she'd gone because it had been a joy to watch him work.

Every tiny nerve, every muscle bundle was carefully lined up and held with the finest sutures, and by the time he'd finished the patient's arm looked almost normal.

'That's amazing,' she said, and he smiled wryly.

'Just doing my job, Livvy, and it was a clean cut. She'll always have a scar, that can't be avoided, but hopefully she'll have full function of all the muscles and nerves, given time. And it's her right arm, so it matters even more. At least we seem to have got all the glass out of her, and once she's come round and she's stable she'll have a CT scan to check for random fragments that we've missed, because she's peppered with it and we're bound to have missed something.' He stripped off his gloves and gown, peeled off his mask and hat and lobbed them in the bin. 'So, what are you doing now?'

She glanced up at the theatre clock. 'I was going to go and see if that boutique had any dresses for Amber, but it might be closed.'

'Are you still happy to do that?'

She stared at him in astonishment. 'Of course I am! I promised her, Matt. I can't go back on that, and I wouldn't want to.'

'So it's just me, then, that you've got a problem with.'

His eyes were unguarded now, and she could see the hurt in them. Hurt she'd caused.

'It's not you, Matt. It's just—I'm always a bit antsy coming up to my mammogram. It brings it all back, makes me nervous.'

'So why not just say that? Why give me all the other excuses?'

'Because I don't want you to be hurt.'

His soft huff of laughter drifted over her silently, but he didn't answer. He didn't need to, because she was hurting him anyway and she could see it in his eyes.

'Go on, go and see if the boutique's still open, and let me know how you get on. I need to go into Recovery and deal with my patient.'

'OK. And thanks again for letting me assist. It was amazing.'

'You're welcome. Call me later.'

'I will.'

It was still open, and the proprietor was wonderful.

'I'm looking for a new favourite dress for a friend's little daughter,' she explained, 'and she hates pink and she doesn't want anything with a unicorn on it.'

The woman laughed and led her through a doorway to the back of the shop.

'There you are. We have some very pretty

summer party dresses for little girls, and there are lots that aren't pink and don't have unicorns,' she said, and showed Livvy a whole rail to choose from.

Some were incredibly fancy and fragile, others much more robust and equally pretty. And as the woman had said, there were lots that weren't pink and she didn't see a single unicorn.

'Oh, they're gorgeous!' she said. 'I'll need to bring her.'

'Of course you will. How big is she?'

'Oh.' She waved her hand up and down, trying to guess. 'So high? I'm not sure. She's five in September, and she's quite slender and leggy. And she needs growing room.'

'OK. I'm sure we'll find something. Do you have a budget?'

She shook her head. 'No. My only criterion is something she can wear more often than the one covered in fine net that she's outgrown and hasn't worn nearly enough to make her happy!'

'That's easy. Bring her when you can.'

'Thursday afternoon? I finish work early then.'

'That's fine. I'll look forward to meeting her. Will her mother be coming?'

Livvy swallowed. 'No, that's why I'm doing this. She doesn't have a mother. She died.'

'Oh, how sad,' the woman said softly. 'We'll have to find her something really special.'

By the time she'd picked Amber up from Matt's house on Thursday afternoon the little girl was positively fizzing with excitement, and the moment she saw the rows of dresses hanging up her eyes were like saucers.

'They're all so pretty!'

'I've pulled a few out for you,' the proprietor said, handing Livvy half a dozen hangers, and they went into the dressing room and Amber tried them all on.

Some were too tight, some too loose, one too short, but then there was one that fitted perfectly but still allowed room for growth, without a trace of pink or a single unicorn, and yet delicately pretty and made of pure, soft cotton with a cotton lining.

It even had a matching cotton cardigan in the exact same soft slate blue as Amber's eyes, with pearly buttons and a picot edging, and watching Amber's delighted reaction when she saw herself in the mirror, Livvy felt her eyes well with tears.

'I think we're probably going to take this one,' she said to the lady, and she smiled.

'I had a feeling you might say that. It's a good choice. It's machine washable, too, and it's pre-shrunk.' She lowered her voice. 'There is another one, which is in the sale, and if she's about to start school she's likely to get lots of party invitations. It's not as dressy, probably not a "favourite" dress, but I think it might suit her.'

It did, and Amber loved it, too, but her little face was troubled.

'If I have this one, does it mean I can't have the other one?'

Livvy shook her head. 'No, sweetheart. It means you can have a favourite dress for parties and more special occasions, and another favourite dress for when it's not quite so important.'

'I can have both?' she squealed, bubbling over with excitement, and Livvy scooped her up and hugged her. Her little arms snaked around her neck, clinging tight, and then she squirmed to be put down and rushed back over to the mirror for another look.

Livvy turned to the saleswoman, surprised to see tears in her eyes, and she felt the prickling echo of them in her own.

'Well, I think that's a success,' the woman said briskly, and Livvy smiled at her.

'I think so, too. Thank you so, so much.'

'It's the least I could do,' she said, and busied herself with wrapping the dresses in tissue.

* * *

'They're beautiful. Thank you so much, Livvy. What do I owe you?'

'Nothing! They're a present.'

'I can't let you do that—'

'Yes, you can. Please. It was a pleasure, just to see the look on her face.'

He let out a little huff of laughter and gave up, pulling her into his arms and hugging her. 'You're a star, do you know that?'

'Absolutely,' she said lightly, but her eyes were glittering and he could tell just from looking at her that she'd found the whole thing very moving.

Such a simple thing, and yet not, because she'd probably never have a daughter of her own, not even a stepdaughter if she stuck to her guns. And that would be a tragedy. He swallowed the lump in his throat and hugged her again.

'I've missed you. We need to make another date.'

'Not yet. I'm working all weekend, and I've got to go to the Audley on Monday for my mammogram.'

'I thought you were working in London before?'

'I was, but after I was diagnosed I switched to the Audley so I could be at home for my treatment. It seemed sensible. But maybe later in the week?'

He nodded. 'I'll ask my mother if she can have the children. How about Friday? I'm not working on Saturday so I can stay over.'

'Friday's fine. I'm not working on Saturday, either. Talk to your mother and let me know.'

The weekend was hellish, but she went over to her parents' on Sunday evening after her shift ended and spent the night with them, then went into the hospital for her mammogram and met up with her mother again for lunch before driving home.

It would be two weeks before she got the result, so she put it out of her mind and tackled her overdue chores. She did a load of laundry and hung it out to dry in the conservatory, blitzed the house, watered the garden and then sat down on the bench with a cold drink just as Matt phoned.

'Hi, how are you?'

'Fine. I've been doing housework, which is deadly dull. How about you?'

He chuckled, which made her smile. 'I'm fine. Amber insisted on wearing her second favourite dress to go round to my mother's for lunch yesterday, and she was distraught because Charlie spilt his drink over it, but d'you know what? It's come out of the washing machine looking as good as new, so I just wanted to thank you again, because it was a brilliant choice and if it had been ruined, life wouldn't have been worth living.'

She laughed at that, wondering how stressed he'd been, visualising the tears and hysteria from Amber.

'Does she know it's OK?'

'Oh, yes. It's back in her wardrobe and she's happy again. So how did the mammogram go?'

'Oh, hellish as ever. I call it the crusher, but it's fine, it's saved my life once, I have no issues with it. My parents send their love, by the way. I spent the night with them and had lunch with Mum today.'

'How are they?'

'Fine.' Apart from worrying about her and quizzing her about her relationship with him, but she wasn't going to tell him that.

'Did they give you a hard time about me?'

She laughed. Apparently she didn't need to tell him. 'Only a little. I told them about taking Amber shopping, and they seemed to think that was a bit serious. I told them it wasn't but they looked as if they didn't believe me.'

He didn't answer that, just grunted, told her his mother could babysit on Friday and then changed the subject to a patient he'd had in a while ago who'd come back for further surgery. 'I've got to take him to Theatre again tomorrow. I wondered if you'd like to scrub in. It could be quite interesting.'

'I'd love to, but I'll have to see how busy it is. I don't suppose James will take kindly to me messing off in the middle of a shift.'

Ludicrously busy was the answer.

Far too busy to leave the department, too busy even for a proper break, just a snatched sandwich or a gulp of water between patients, and it set the tone for the rest of the week.

Still, she'd see him on Friday, and they spoke in the evening a couple of times.

And then on Friday, she got back to the house to find a recall letter from the breast clinic, and her world went into meltdown.

CHAPTER TEN

SHE WASN'T ANSWERING her phone.

There had to be a perfectly good reason, like she was watering the garden or she'd nipped out to the corner shop or she was in the shower or drying her hair—any one of a dozen perfectly plausible reasons, but he had a cold, sick feeling in the pit of his stomach and he knew—he just *knew*—there was something wrong.

He'd been trying to get hold of her for half an hour. Nobody dried their hair for that long. And the last time his calls hadn't been picked up—

Stop it! She's not dead.

But the fear in his gut was growing, and there was nothing he could do about it because his mother wasn't feeling well so she couldn't babysit, so he had no way of getting to Livvy to see if she was all right.

Unless…

He spotted Ed on the clifftop, heading home with the dog, and he ran out and hailed him.

'Can you do me a massive favour? Can you babysit the kids for ten minutes? They're in bed asleep but Mum can't make it, she's not well, and I can't get hold of Livvy and I'm supposed to have picked her up twenty minutes ago, and I'm a bit worried.'

'Yes, of course I can. Go. Ring me if there's a problem.'

He nodded, dived back in, picked up his keys and drove straight to her house. Her car wasn't outside the front and her bedroom window was closed, as if she hadn't got home.

Odd. If she'd been held up at work she would have called him, or got someone else to.

He peered through the letter box and saw nothing, so he tried her phone again, and he could hear it ringing.

She must have left it behind—except she never left her phone behind. And the door from the kitchen to the conservatory was open.

The garden. She was in the garden.

His shoulders dropping with relief, he drove round to the back of the house, hitched up on the kerb and got out.

'Livvy?'

Silence, apart from a familiar noise, the slight, rhythmic creak of the swing. And she hadn't answered him, even though she must have heard, but at least she was alive. He grabbed the top of the gate, hauled himself up and dropped to the ground on the other side.

Her car was there, neatly parked in the car port, and he ducked under the wisteria into the garden and found her huddled on the bench, her eyes vacant and red-rimmed, and his heart turned over.

'Hey, what's happened?' he asked softly, and she looked up and met his eyes and he felt sick.

He sat down and gathered her up against his chest, her body resisting, shudders running through it, and lying on the floor at her feet was a crumpled letter from the Audley breast clinic.

They found something.

He felt the air leave his lungs in a rush, and he cradled her head against his shoulder and rocked her gently.

'Did you get a recall?'

She nodded. 'They found something,' she said in a tiny voice. 'I have to go back.'

'When?'

'Monday.'

Damn. Why was it the weekend? Why was it always the weekend?

'Matt, why are you here?'

He pressed a kiss to her hair, his heart welling over. 'Because I was supposed to be taking you out for dinner,' he said gently, 'but my mother's not well and I've been trying to ring you and you didn't pick up.'

'Oh. Sorry. I forgot,' she said, her voice hollow.

She was in shock, her body cold and stiff, her lips bloodless.

'That's OK. Come on, let's get you some things, you're coming back to my house for the weekend.'

'No. Just leave me—'

'No. I'm not leaving you, Livvy, never again. You're coming back with me. What do you need? Underwear, toothbrush, deodorant, clothes—'

'Tamoxifen,' she said, and then a sob tore its way out of her body and he squeezed his eyes shut and held her.

She didn't give in, though, just crushed it all down as he guessed she always did and lifted her head and sniffed.

'Matt, I'm OK, really. I don't want—I can't—'

'Yes, you can. Come on, get up and we'll go and get you some things together and then we'll go back to mine so we can talk.'

'I don't want to talk. There's nothing to say.'

'There's a lot to say, a lot I should already

have said, but that's fine, we've got time. Come on.'

He got up and tugged her gently to her feet, gathered her things together in the bedroom and bathroom, picked up her bag, locked up the house and took her home.

Ed was sitting in the porch by the open door, the dog lying at his feet, and he took one look at Matt's face when he got out of the car and stood up.

'Anything I can do?' he asked quietly, but there wasn't so he shook his head.

'No. Thanks for staying. I can't talk now.'

Ed nodded, told him to call if he needed anything and left him to it.

'Come on, Livvy. Come inside.'

He was going to nag her until she went, so she got out of the car, her body working on autopilot, and he shepherded her into the house and took her up to his bedroom. She crawled onto the bed without a word, and he lay down and pulled her into his arms.

She resisted for a moment, then burrowed into him, clinging to him like a lifeline, too weak to fight it any longer because she needed him so much and it was all going to go horribly wrong—

'Hey, it'll be all right,' he murmured.

'No, it won't. It's come back, I know it has. Why am I here? You don't need this, Matt. You don't need me—'

'Yes, I do. I love you, Livvy, and I know you love me, too.'

Her eyes welled with tears because this was what she'd been dreading, the moment when it all imploded. 'No! No, don't say that. You can't say that. You can't love me, I won't let you.'

'You can't stop me, my darling. I love you, and I don't have a choice about that—and I don't want a choice. I don't want anybody else, I want you.'

'But I could die—'

'Yes, you could. We all could. We all will. I still want you. I still love you, and I always will, for as long as I have you, and that's not negotiable because there's nothing I can do about it. You mean the world to me, and whatever happens in the future I'm here for you. We can do this, Livvy. We can face this together, whatever it is, whatever they've found. It's probably nothing, but even if it isn't, I'm here, and I'm staying.'

'No. That's not fair to you.'

'Life isn't fair. If it was fair Jules wouldn't have died, and my father wouldn't have got cancer, and I wouldn't have a job and neither would you, because we wouldn't be needed.

It's not fair, but it's what we have, and we have to make the best of every single moment of it, and that means staying together.'

'But what about the children? What about Amber—?' Her voice cracked, and she felt his arms tighten.

'Let's not worry about them yet, let's get you sorted first and find out what's going on and deal with it, OK? Because it's probably nothing.'

She sat up and sniffed, and he stuffed a tissue into her hand and she blew her nose and lay down again, her head on his shoulder, determined not to cry.

'I keep telling myself that. It's happened before. I had a cyst and they got all excited about it, but—you know, it's just there, the threat, it's always there, and I ignore it and just get on with life and then it sneaks up and bites me when I'm not looking. That's why I was so crabby, because I knew it could happen, but I never expected it—'

'I know. I never expected Jules to die, I didn't expect to lose my father in his early sixties, but that doesn't mean I wish I'd never known them, never loved them. Marry me, Livvy. Let me be here for you. Let me love you.'

Her heart turned over, the longing to say

yes overwhelming her. 'No. I can't. I won't. I'm not going to marry you because you feel sorry for me, or because you're lonely, or because you want to atone for not being there for Jules when she died—'

'That's not why I'm asking you to marry me! I don't feel sorry for you. I *hate* what's happened to you, what's happening now, but it's not pity. And I don't want to marry you because I'm lonely, and it's certainly not because I feel guilty about Jules, because I don't. There was nothing anyone could have done. Even if I'd been there, she would probably have died, or at best been in a vegetative state, and she would have hated that. I want to marry you because *I love you.*'

She shook her head, trying not to listen, shutting out the words she couldn't bear to hear because she wanted it so much, wanted him so much—

'Please don't love me, Matt, please. I can't bear the thought of you being hurt.'

'Then don't hurt me,' he said simply. 'Let me in, Livvy. Let me help you, let me be there for you, love me back, because that's all I need. I don't need guarantees, I don't need certainty, I just need you, for as long as I can have you, whether that's six weeks or sixty years.'

She turned her head and stared at him.

'Sixty years?'

'Why not?'

'You'll be ninety-six.'

'Yeah. If I'm lucky. I'm working on the principle I could live that long, so I'm taking care of myself, but I don't expect it, I'm not banking on it, and I'm not putting anything off until tomorrow because it may not be there.'

He stroked her hair, his fingers gentle as he brushed it away from her face.

'I know the future's uncertain, but you're denying us the certainty of happiness for the uncertain possibility that your cancer could come back, maybe now, maybe years down the line, maybe never. I'll take that risk, Livvy. I'll take it hands down over losing you for nothing, because I love you,' he murmured, and then his lips found hers, his kiss tender and—steadfast?

Odd word, but it popped into her head and made her want to cry, because that was just him all over.

'Make love to me,' she whispered, and he got up and locked the bedroom door and came back to her, pulling her to her feet and kissing her again, his mouth coaxing, tender.

He undressed her slowly, and she turned her head and looked out at the darkening sky and silver sea beyond the open doors.

'Aren't you going to close the curtains?'

'No. Nobody can see in. We're too high, and anyway, the lights aren't on.'

He stripped off his clothes and led her back to the bed, his mouth finding hers again, his touch gentle. His body gleamed silver in the moonlight, and she ran her hand over his skin, feeling the texture of it, more alive than she'd ever been because this moment was so precious, and she wanted to store every moment of it, to save it in her memory bank. Just in case…

She cradled his face in her hands, kissing him back a little desperately, and she felt the nip of his teeth on her lip, the heat of his breath as he explored her body, wringing every drop of sensation out of her.

Their lovemaking was touched with sweetness, but also desperation, a poignant tenderness and honesty that unravelled her, and when it was over he lifted his head and gently wiped the tears from her cheeks.

'Now tell me you don't love me,' he said unevenly, and she bit her lip and turned her head away.

'Come on, Livvy. Tell me you don't love me as much as I love you. Go on, Livvy. Say it.'

'I can't say it.'

'Why? Why can't you say it?'

She turned her head back and stared straight into his eyes.

'Because I do love you,' she whispered, and his eyes filled and he gathered her into his arms and cradled her against his heart.

'Thank you. Thank you for being honest with me at last. I love you, too, Livvy. So very, very much. And we can do this, my love. We'll get there, somehow. It'll be all right.'

Would it? She doubted it. She'd given up on miracles a long, long time ago—but then she hadn't had Matt in her life.

Could she let him love her?

Could she let herself love him, and his children?

Maybe he was right and they didn't have a choice, not about any of it.

He lifted his hand and stroked the hair back off her face. 'Are you OK?'

She nodded. 'I just want it over. I want to know, whatever it is. It's the not knowing that's so hard.'

'I know. Have you eaten?'

'Eaten?' she said, as if he'd asked her if she could fly, and he laughed softly.

'Yes, eaten. I'm starving. Do you fancy a sandwich?'

'Have you got any hummus and celery or peppers or whatever?'

'I think so. Why don't you have a shower while I go and raid the fridge?'

He closed the curtains then and pulled on his underwear and left her to it, padding downstairs in bare feet to see what he could find, and a few minutes later she appeared, her hair wrapped in a towel, wearing the shirt he'd taken off with the cuffs turned back, and looking unbearably lovely.

'That shirt's never looked so good,' he said with a smile, and she smiled back at him, her eyes sad and wounded still but a little less afraid.

'Did you find hummus?'

'I've found all sorts of things. Shall we eat here?'

She nodded and settled herself on the bar stool. 'Matt, I don't think I should stay. What about the children?'

'What about them? You can use the spare room if you want, but I don't think it's necessary. They're going to have to get used to it.'

'No. Matt, no. I can't do this to you—'

'You're not doing it to me.'

'Or them.'

He looked away, his heart sinking.

'Let's just get through the weekend, eh? I'll call the hospital in the morning and clear my diary for Monday. What time's your appointment?'

'Two, but—'

'OK. I can do that.'

'You don't need to come!'

'Yes, I do. I've said I will, and I will. You're not driving yourself all that way. Do your parents know?'

'No, and I'm not telling them, so please don't.'

'OK. That's fair enough, there's no need to spook them. You can talk to them afterwards, when it's all fine.'

'If.'

'When. Here, have something to eat.'

She didn't know what he told the children the next morning, but Charlie just ran around in his own little world, driving cars along the walls and screeching round the garden making aeroplane noises, and Amber sat at the table in a shady corner of the patio with a colouring book and some pencils and watched her out of the corner of her eye.

She was sitting on Matt's bench hoping that the sun would thaw the cold place inside her, and he'd gone in to make them all a drink and a snack when Amber got up and came over to her, wriggling up onto the bench beside her.

'Why are you sad?' she asked softly, and Livvy felt her heart squeeze.

'I'm not sad, sweetheart, I'm just a little worried about something.'

'Are you sure you're not sad?'

'Yes, I'm sure. What are you colouring?'

'A butterfly. Do you want to help me?'

Yes, but was it a good idea? To bond with her, and let Amber get closer to her—just in case…?

'Would you like me to?'

'Yes, please. It's very beautiful. It'll make you feel better.'

It did, oddly. Not the colouring, although concentrating hard on it was nicely distracting, but the quiet company of this gentle and affectionate little girl was very soothing, and they spent a large part of the day sitting side by side over the colouring book while Matt entertained Charlie and kept supplying them with drinks and snacks.

And that night, after the children were in bed and they'd eaten the curry he'd made for them, he took her to bed and made love to her again, and yet again his gentleness made her cry.

'I'm sorry. I just…'

'I know. It's OK,' he murmured, and held her until she fell asleep.

* * *

On Sunday they borrowed the Shackletons'
dog, Molly, and went for a walk, down to the
harbour and along the river wall. Molly was
too big for either of the children to hold, so
Matt had her on her lead and walked with
Charlie, and Amber slipped her hand into
Livvy's and skipped along beside her behind
them, pointing out the gaunt ribs of old boats
that had sunk in the mud at the edge of the
river.

'Daddy said they might have been smug-
glers,' she said, eyes wide, and Livvy found
herself smiling.

They had lunch outside the pub overlooking the harbour, with Molly begging shame-
lessly, and then walked back up to the house
and handed her back to her family, and somehow the rest of the day crawled slowly by.

She couldn't sleep that night, and while Matt
was asleep she put his shirt on again and crept
out through the doors and sat on the balcony,
listening to the faint, distant sound of the sea
sucking on the shingle as the tide receded.
It was soothing and rhythmical, and if she'd
thought she could do it without waking him
she would have let herself out and gone down
there.

But then he would have woken and been

worried, and he didn't deserve that, so she sat and stared into the darkness, watching the lights on a ship moving slowly across her field of view, until finally a pale silver light crept over the edge of the sea and the sky began to lighten.

Monday.

She'd thought it would never come, and now it had, she wished it hadn't.

She heard a faint sound and turned, and he was standing there in the doorway, his hand held out to her. She took it and let him lead her back to bed.

She took the whole day off work, but Matt was in clinic until twelve, which meant she was alone in her house all morning, and of course she was swamped with nerves and dread and negative thoughts that wouldn't leave her alone.

'It'll be nothing,' she kept telling herself, but then Matt pulled up at the gate and she walked out of the front door into his arms and burst into tears.

'I can't do this,' she sobbed, but he just held her for a moment until she'd pulled herself together, handed her a tissue and put her in the car, then slid behind the wheel and reached over to give her hand a reassuring squeeze.

* * *

They walked into the breast clinic, she gave her name and the receptionist smiled at her.

'I'll just get the breast-care nurse to come and talk to you,' she said, and she felt the blood drain from her face because this was what had happened before, when she had been diagnosed.

'Livvy? Come and sit down, you're white as a sheet.'

He led her to a chair and sat with his arm around her, and then the breast-care nurse came out, all smiles.

'Hi, Livvy. Don't worry, there are just a few little dots in your left breast and the consultant wants a closer look. They look like cysts, like you had before, but he just wants to be sure, OK? We won't keep you long.'

She nodded, and her hand found its way into Matt's and clung like a limpet until she was called in.

Then called again, and then again, because the consultant still wasn't happy that he'd seen enough.

'I'm sorry. Hopefully that'll be it,' the radiographer said, and she went back out into the waiting room and Matt gathered her into his arms.

'OK?'

'Sort of. You know those olive presses they have to squeeze the oil out?' she said, and he chuckled and dropped a kiss on her lips.

'I'm sorry.'

'Don't be. It's not your fault.'

She was then sent off for an ultrasound, and finally the breast-care nurse showed them into the consultant's office and his smile told her everything she wanted to know.

'Hi, Livvy, sorry about that, but it's good news, it's all fine. Just cysts, the one you had before and a couple of new ones. They're all tiny, but the one that was there before hasn't grown, so we'll keep monitoring them, but I'm absolutely certain they're not cancer, so you can relax.'

Beside her she heard Matt's huff of relief, but she wasn't convinced. It couldn't be that easy—

'Are you sure?'

He smiled patiently. 'Yes, Livvy, I'm sure. You're fine. I'm signing you off. I still want an eye kept on those cysts, but as far as I'm concerned your cancer's gone, there's no sign of it anywhere, the oncology team have discharged you—you're done.'

'And the tamoxifen?'

He shrugged. 'You've had it for five years. You could keep taking it, or you could stop.

It's up to you, but it's probably not necessary any more. You're at no more risk now than anybody else.'

'And my fertility?'

He shook his head. 'I can't answer that, because it's not that straightforward and everyone's different, but what I would say is make sure you don't get pregnant for at least six months to allow the tamoxifen to clear your system, and I would recommend you never use any hormonal contraception. Apart from that, all I can say is go away and enjoy your life.'

He stood up and shook her hand, and then Matt's, pausing with a puzzled frown.

'I remember you. Matt Hunter, isn't it?'

'Yes. I remember you, too. Good to see you again—especially with good news.'

He smiled. 'Take care of her. She's very special to us.'

His arm closed round her shoulders, holding her firmly against his side. 'Don't worry, I will. She's very special to me, too.'

He led her out of the room, down the corridor and into his arms.

'I'm OK,' she said, and burst into tears.

He held her close, his eyes firmly shut, somehow keeping his own emotions in check, and then when she lifted her head he kissed away her tears and handed her a tissue.

'You have an unending supply of these,' she said, and he chuckled.

'I do. I have small children. I also have shares in the company.'

'Seriously?'

'No, of course not,' he said, laughing, and her lips tipped into the first proper smile he'd seen for days.

'Will your parents be at home?'

'Maybe. It's Monday, they both finish pretty early.'

'Let's go and see. There's something I want to ask your father, and you need to tell them you've been signed off.'

'I do. They'll be relieved.'

No doubt. He knew he was, but it wasn't over yet because he still had to convince Livvy to let him into her life, and if there was one thing he knew about her, it was just how stubborn she could be, but maybe he could marshal an ally.

They were there, and she walked into the kitchen and told them the good news, and the relief on their faces was a joy to see.

They broke out the champagne—the bottle he'd given Oliver for his birthday, Matt noticed—and he and Livvy had a tiny glass each, him because he was driving, her because she didn't drink now, but this was different, and it needed toasting.

Then the conversation moved on, and he caught Oliver's eye.

'Can I have a word? I've got a patient who you've seen in the past, and there's something I want to run by you. Can we go into your study?'

'What was that all about?'

'Oh, nothing much. Just a mutual patient. Sorry we had to rush away, but Mum's still not feeling amazing and I need to get back to put the kids to bed.'

'That's fine. You can drop me home.'

'No. We need to go straight to mine. I'll get you a taxi home, but maybe we can have supper first. Or you could stay?'

'That's becoming a habit.'

'Not all habits are bad.'

He reached out a hand, and she threaded her fingers through his and he lifted them to his lips. 'Feeling better now?'

She rested her head back and smiled contentedly. 'Much. Tired, though. I spent rather too long sitting on your balcony last night.'

'I know. I was watching you. Why don't you close your eyes and go to sleep? I'll wake you when we get there.'

Amber ran to her when they walked in, wrapping her arms around her hips and hugging her.

'You're here again! Can we do some more colouring?'

'Darling, it's your bedtime and anyway, I expect Livvy might be tired,' Matt's mother said, her eyes concerned, but Livvy smiled at her.

'I'm fine. Really.'

'Really fine?' she asked, and Livvy realised Matt must have told her.

'Yes. I'm *really* fine,' she said, and then watched as Jane's eyes welled with tears.

'Well, that's wonderful. I'm so pleased. Right, if you don't need me, I'll go home and leave you all to it.'

Matt kissed her. 'Yes, sure. Thank you so much for today. I'm sorry we're so late.'

'Don't be.'

She kissed his cheek, then hugged Livvy and left, and Matt told her to find herself a drink and took the children upstairs.

He was an age, even though he didn't bath them, and sitting in the kitchen near the open door she could hear him and Amber talking. She couldn't hear what they were saying, but there was a little shriek of excitement at one point, and he shushed her, and then she heard the door open and Amber say, 'Please let me ask her!'

'No, Amber. It's better coming from me. Go back to bed.'

She heard a little protest, then his deep murmur, then his footsteps running lightly down the stairs. He came into the kitchen, pushed the door to and walked towards her, his face solemn, and she frowned in puzzlement.

'What was that about? What's better coming from you?'

She didn't know what she was expecting—another dress-buying favour, a trip out, a manicure? But he looked too serious for that.

'Something Amber apparently feels very strongly about, but I thought exposing you to her charm offensive would be emotional blackmail, and I didn't think that was fair because, yes, it affects her and Charlie, but ultimately it's between us, and I need you to feel you can be honest.'

He took her hand, and then to her surprise he went down on one knee, and her heart hitched.

'Are you offering me a piggy-back down a mountain?' she asked, trying to lighten it, but he just shook his head and smiled.

'No. I'm offering you a piggy-back through

life, Livvy, because whoever we are, whatever's going on, there are always ups and downs, and we need someone to do that for us, to keep us going when the going gets tough, to lift us up when we're down—you could always return the favour.'

'I don't think I could lift you,' she said unsteadily, but he shook his head, his eyes tender.

'You lift me all the time. In the short time I've known you, you've made me happy in a way I thought I'd never be happy again. You've brought me so much hope, so much joy, so much love, and I want you to give me—to give the children—a chance to give that back to you, to give you some of what you've given us. Will you marry me, Olivia? Not because I feel sorry for you, or because I'm lonely, or because I feel guilty, but because I love you, with all my heart, and I can't bear the thought of not having you in my life, in our lives, because you'll make them so much richer. And I know it won't be easy, marriage never is, you have to take the rough with the smooth, but that's what life's about, and I want to share mine with you for as long as we have, whatever happens and whatever it brings us.'

He lifted her hand, holding it flat against his heart, and his eyes were burning with love.

'Marry me, Livvy. I need you, I love you, and I don't want to spend another day without you. Please don't make me. And if that sounds like emotional blackmail, it isn't meant to. It's just the plain, honest truth.'

She couldn't speak. The tears were welling so fast his beautiful eyes were going out of focus, and she could hardly breathe.

'Y-yes,' she said, and then, just in case that wasn't clear enough, she said it again, lifting his hand to her lips and kissing it. 'Yes. Yes, I'll marry you, I don't want to spend another day without you, either. I love you. All of you, so very, very much.'

Behind him the door opened, and Amber ran in and hugged him.

'I *told* you she'd say yes, Daddy!'

Livvy laughed and swiped away the tears that were streaming down her cheeks, and he got to his feet, Amber in his arms, and handed her a tissue.

'I think I might need more than one. Maybe you should buy the company.'

'Or stop making you cry. That might be better.'

'Not if I'm crying with happiness.'

'Maybe not. Amber, say goodnight to Livvy

and then go up to bed, please. It's way past your bedtime and we have things to talk about.'

'Like the wedding?' she said excitedly.

Livvy smiled at her, knowing how much the little girl was going to love helping them plan the wedding. 'We can talk about the wedding later, Amber,' she said gently. 'There'll be lots of time to do that.'

'But can't we do it now?' she pleaded.

'No. It's late and you're tired and it's time for bed,' he said, and Livvy bent down and kissed her, then holding her hand she led her upstairs and into her room, tucked her into bed and kissed her goodnight.

'I'm glad you said yes. I really wanted you to be my new mummy,' Amber told her, clinging to her hand, and she smiled, her eyes welling again.

'I'm glad I said yes, too, and I'll do my best to be a good mummy to you and Charlie.'

'Can I call you Mummy?'

Oh, heavens. Livvy's eyes overflowed, and she blinked hard. 'I think we need to talk to Daddy about that,' she said, wondering if he might have strong feelings about it.

She kissed Amber again, then stood up and turned, to find Matt standing there, his face awash with emotion.

'Night-night, little one,' he murmured, bending down to kiss his daughter, and then he turned and ushered Livvy out of the room.

'Finally,' he said, shutting the door, and taking her hand he led her through his bedroom and onto the balcony, turned her into his arms and stared down into her eyes.

'You see what I mean about the charm offensive?'

'No. She's delightful. She even—did you hear? She asked if she can call me Mummy.'

'I know. And, yes, of course she can, if you don't mind.'

'Mind? Why should I mind? I was worried about you. You don't feel—well, that it's not my place?'

He shook his head. 'No. She needs a mummy, and I'm only too happy that it's going to be you. But don't be fooled. She can be a tiny bit manipulative. Are you sure you don't feel pressganged?'

She shook her head, unable to keep the smile off her face. 'I don't feel press-ganged. I just feel wanted.'

'Oh, you're certainly wanted, my darling.' He dropped a tiny kiss on the end of her nose. 'You need to phone your parents and put them out of their misery.'

'How do they know—? Oh, you sneaky

thing! That's what you wanted to talk to him about!'

'Of course. You have to do things properly. But there's something I have to do first before I let you go,' he murmured, a slow, sexy smile playing around his mouth as he bent his head and kissed her...

* * * * *

If you enjoyed this story, check out these other great reads from Caroline Anderson

One Night, One Unexpected Miracle
Their Own Little Miracle
Bound by Their Babies
The Midwife's Longed-For Miracle

All available now!